DIORAMAS

— A NOVEL —

BLAIR AUSTIN

DZANC
BOOKS

DZANC BOOKS

2580 Craig Rd.
Ann Arbor, MI 48103
www.dzancbooks.org

First Edition: March 2023
Cover design by Matthew Revert
Interior design byMichelle Dotter
ISBN: 9781950539758

Printed in the United States of America

10   9   8   7   6   5   4   3   2   1

For Edward Dorn
In Memoriam

book i: animals

I: THE MUSEUM

The Bower

HERE IS A GLASS CASE, green dark like a bottle, enclosing the interior boughs of a tree (a simulated hornbeam, I think). On the branches perch hundreds of canaries taken out of the mines. The lemon coats are muddied with coal dust and appear oily. Their eyes stare.

Some specimens have decayed. They have been taken out of the diorama. One can see where they used to be; they seem to have been used to make repairs on others. Up close, the birds have the stitched-together look of people living under bridges who have lost all sense of their surroundings. Glass beads painted to look like the berries of the mountain ash bulk in cascading clusters, striking the viewer as odd because canaries don't eat them, being strictly seed-eaters. Many of the birds have been eaten by mice and dust mite larvae, which have caused them to slip their skins and to show their cork molds on which wine stains can just be seen if you look closely.

Affixed to the case frame, a little plaque lists the names of the birds and the dates they tipped over in their cages. The time notation is flipped—at first you can't tell the year from the month. All engraved with almost maniacal care, in wiggles and squiggles that must have taken hours to complete. Loo-Loo. Chapper. Tip-Tip. Little Jim. Big Jim. And so forth.

The birds made up of other birds have been given the names of all those salvaged birds whose parts made them up, in parentheses. Only in one case there is a single name, Sally, with the phrase, "et al.," to signify the unnamed.

7

If one looks closely, there is a nest in the back with three, pea-sized eggs inside. Leaning against the nest rim is a single penny, too dim to communicate the year of its minting, fallen or possibly placed there in an act of Coining: the placing of a coin on the body of deceased birds, a practice done for good luck, still done to this day.

This diorama, a memorial from a time when people went down in the mines, is similar to the War Pigeons in their case, further on, who carried messages in battle and were the common target of the enemy. When telegraph lines were cut, the birds were released. They fled through the air to reach the dovecote under enemy fire, a compulsion that produced no shortage of heroes, unquote, whose toughness resembled courage. Although, whereas the pigeons were driven by fear, by a force eerie as a magnet within them, like a bow continuously bent, the canaries, for their part, waited. They waited for the muffling of sound, the passage narrowing in the lamps, and the euphoria of the gas. The pigeons, just a ways down the hall, stand with wings folded, their heads held in the alert posture of children who have graduated from private schools.

Both these dioramas are slated for removal. Perhaps to be restored. That the canaries went into the dark is the suggestion. And that they are now in the bower...

The Reef

THE REEF'S OUTCROPPINGS CURVE INTO the distance. The shelves of rock, too, take the blanket of the velvet monstrosities, with their wiggles, their hairs. Over the carpeting of what seems like every pliant shape (tubes transparent, fingers with a bowel-like bend to them) float the creatures that make their home here. I haven't handy the exact figures, but a quantity of resin, serving as seawater and tinted with the proper, cheese-hued greens has been poured over the deeply delicate ware of the ceramic coral. The glazes are the prime wonder.

Schools, of course, swarm. But the fish lack the mirror as it breaks, that kineticism of aquariums. In this diorama they seem not to need their sudden shifts, nor to mind. Hundreds of schools, of hundreds of different species, over-monitored by a few climax predator species, among them the poor sharks. A swallow whale. Heaps of coins flash next to dark ropes, dark heaves of no definite shape, the green mouth swallowing the black, galloping chains out of the same oval.

It's a bit much.

Slide please, Jeffrey.

Workers installed the littlest creatures—shy in the coral—while in harness, tweezing them with a dab of epoxy (a special formulation that gave off no heat at peak viscosity, nor as it cooled, so as not to disrupt any of the fine coloration). The reef accepted this quietly. The resin (we are talking of the resin bulk) piled against the glass of the viewing window, folding a transparent body, pooling over delicate life, and then began to solidify without destroying all it engulfed.

The floor girders are stout, indeed, to accept such weight on the eleventh floor.

Note, there are no swimmers. No divers. As yet, the sun shines, but since the lighting is designed to bring the varying levels, all the way to the quiet swarm, and later in the evening a moon to guide and to view, one can always expect this to change. Change is the medium of a reef. The difference comes on slow.

This clump of underwater shrubbery issues into the gloom an almost human appendage to snatch a fish, equally odd-shapen. We cast an eye over the ordinary wonders, which almost seem to move, to catch weight and turn their mechanical parts: the frozen palace hinges, their knobs of glass beings, each with a flower trapped inside, each with a hand turning itself over, to grow a pale door of tentacles. This will go on forever, as after a blast, a neighborhood lies flattened but a living room in some outcrop balcony is sheltered, is preserved with its ash trap and tchotchke, a rug of imitation hair, a lantern of accelerant and globe, its dainty chain on a plumb to the center of all side tables: fingerprints on the glass, tumbler rings still evident where the coaster was missed...the insect hairs of the horsehair cushion, there is some kind of continuity, almost spiritual but which stops just before our understanding.

Whales

A CLOUD OF BLOOD GLOWS red. Our movement along the glass disperses the light. Never, were it not for the explanatory matter, would we guess that this display began long ago, someplace else, at the bottom of the rubble.

A shard of wood: a split oar, the oarlock still attached, drifts toward heaven's reverse, turned 'round for darkness. This clue of a boat, once above, cannot be seen from the other observation windows of the Whale Diorama. Here (lower third window, floor seven), there is simply a vast undersea, a lightening of the green going upward, a darkening going down (we felt we floated), an orange glow as well, as of a sunset or, as some have said, a burning vessel or the furnaces of the whale oil extraction process, or the furnace of the wider world itself, which evoke the familiar sense of the sentries and symbol, "decline"—declension rather than outright, slope and y-intercept at the midway point of the parabola. Why, then, do we not know for sure?

This diorama, you may be aware, dating from before the early city, is over four thousand, six hundred years old, dated by the usual means. It was discovered under the iron and beams, the reinforcing bars like little trachea with a case of the scales, basemented by a catastrophe, and when discovered at the crystalline, southeast corner, glowing, or it seemed to the discoverers—and to thousands of pilgrims, who, earlier prayed to the strange, cubelike structure—they did not know it stretched on and on, both under and far, could not have known. Could not have known. Everything is "Could not have known."

As you know, there are but three such ancient dioramas in existence, one of which contains the hind leg of a dog and the other of which was intended more as an encyclopedic bestiary with all sorts of species displayed on a "mountain side."

The conservation of the Whale Diorama ran the usual track, save the fact that, being encased in that resin (so pervasive, so peculiar to the time before and enabling no picking-over, so air and watertight), everything was perfectly preserved. The worshippers found simply a blue and green projection, like glass, that would warp the light. Little did they know the great diorama that deepened under the rubble. No, it took the South River Flood, and more, to eat away the ground and expose this giant—and to us, quaint—museum as a lens of worship. That fascinating resin, that cool, clean substance that one can say is the very essence of the time before.

The excavation was the work of years done under a temporary roof out of the weather until, one by one, in great slices the diorama of the whale came into the light. To be taken to the warehouses, studied and conserved, restored and reassembled, at last, in the museum.

The seams of the reconstruction had to be flawless.

Each piece, when lifted out and reassembled, is quite smooth. Think of an aspic or the seamless room of an insect in amber (who were indeed the first prisoners of the diorama) or a lovely ordinance gelatin, cut with a wire pulled smooth—no stutters—then placed near as can be to the original before the final fitting of the holding-resin (made of locust gum) like honey that dries clear.

There were hollows where creatures had been dissolved over time. Great cracks, as from some cataclysm, ran through some of the resin, you see. A concussion sudden and total it must have been, and the rainwater trickled down through the collapsed structure. The conservators, to get the outline and detail of what had once dwelled there, filled these voids with dental plaster, which, when set, gave the shape of the creatures whole, every outline and hair, even the divots on the tongue of this individual. And then the great block of resin was sawn through and opened as if on hinges, like a sarcophagus, the whale in dental plaster hoisted out and transported with great care to the workshops. Following this, a selection of the likeliest dye brought out the details on the plaster, which was then painted, and the entire creature took skin, looking exactly as it might have done in the original. The two halves of the resin block were then refitted around the animal and sealed with a twinning-resin, exactly specified to blend so that no evidence of the repair can be seen.

Conservation is an act of despair and also an act of faith. The finished diorama, Window Six. The strained distances, the flecks of the watered world in their cloud-removes. As buildings of murk and passage, growing narrower, the now burgeoning corridor of the balloon's interior, wet with breathing, has gone on, independent. "The sense that some localized portion of the world burns above ice." These are Michaux's, the great dioramist's, words.

Our earlier ship on fire, or furnaces, perhaps, for whale oil. One isn't sure. Some of the charm and the unease comes from the light itself, avoided, yet also coming toward us in the murk, through the timbre, if you will, of the smoke, the unintentional air trapped in these microscopic bubbles like white fleas.

Amateur

ON MY DESK IS A diorama of two theen finches, a female and a
male, yellow with a brown cap. I finished the diorama—to my
dissatisfaction—a week ago and sealed it in a glass box to keep out
the dust. But the dust got in anyway, settling on the moss, which
I'd intended to be wet. After taking it apart and cleaning the moss, I
decided I could spare the materials for a second glass box, to nest the
first, sealing the edges of the wood frame with wax, which I smoothed
with a piece of wood I'd carved for that purpose.

I had found the female finch near W Station on my way to the
museum when I still worked there. I wrapped the creature in my
handkerchief and stored it in my lunch box.

She has pinned a hazelnut under one foot while pecking. Her head
is raised, beak toward breast, for a powerful, downward thrust. Other
hazelnuts, some still in their haired husks, are placed on the moss. I
found them, too—in the woodlot near my apartment. But then on a
whim I changed my mind. I wanted two birds. So I bought a premade
male of the same species at a supply shop, colored blue-yellow, with a
black cap. I took the boxes apart again and put him in.

Dioramas are an expensive hobby.

The theen finch is a ground-dwelling bird, and the male stands on
the moss, its blue sometimes yellow, its yellow sometimes blue. Head
tipped, he scratches the top of his head with a claw. He is an exemplar,
unusually slender in his lines, while the female I tried to prepare is
somewhat lumpy, as if the two had been twins separated at birth and

14

released in different wood lots. In low light, they smear. It is difficult to tell which is which, save by their posture, but as morning comes and my room fills with sunlight, the birds go into themselves, like into a glass of water. Yet when the light is off, and I am near sleep, they are there in the dark.

Playbill

Associate Lecturer H.G. Wiggins
Presents His Last Lecture Series:
The Dioramas of the City
Every Tuesday Evening, 8 PM
Theater Odeon
Museum Annex 2B
Free and Open to the Public

The Theater Odeon

THE THEATER ODEON IS AN acoustic wonder. It is a holdover from the time before sound amplification replaced shouting as a means of being heard in large crowds. The seats of the second and third tiers rise straight up into the plaster. The ceiling curves to meet them, scooping overhead like a shell, and the highest seats lean over the stage, creating a sound trap, a whisper chamber, and there never was a lonelier sight than the old lecturer down there shuffling his papers at the lectern.

Tonight, the heat is immense. The transoms are open, and you can hear the rain. Programs flap, unable to take flight. A strange odor rises: the odor of human skin. The heat shimmers upward through the high vents of cobweb and iron, pouring motes into the city, and if these inferior vents were not there, you could imagine the whole of the theater, lobby and all, heaved free of the slabbing, wrenched from the side of the museum, to rise like a hot air balloon, a pretty skull of glowing scallops and moldings, leaving Lecturer Wiggins alone on the fan-shaped stage.

Way up, at the very top, the molding takes on the astonishing characteristics of a bas-relief. There are godlike heroes, backgrounded by failing suns and spiral clouds of destruction, all scooped and sculpted deeply enough in the plaster to serve as habitation for some fifteen cats. A donor insisted on their presence, and the creatures have been there ever since, stretching here and there, paws hung over the edges of the plaster waterfalls, or leaping from place to place with curvilinear nonchalance according to their whim and social structure.

The old lecturer, adjusting his spectacles, arranges his glass of doctored cranberry juice on the lectern. Even the scratching of his chin can be heard far up, at the top of the theatre. And there is the reverse image of Lecturer Wiggins blinking into the lemon wall of the sconce-light. But he can't see anyone, except at the far edge of the boards: a few indistinct vessels, which are the faces down front merging into that wall, at once made of light and composed of the darkness. The feeling is exactly like going under for surgery. He leans. He grips. Coming toward him, growing more distinct, the edge of the boards (with the black nail holes and the masking tape marking off some performance) grows clear, but never the audience, whose presence he gets by the sound…and there, in the first row, some half-dozen friends who have not abandoned him. From these he gauges the audience—indeed, its very existence—in the new night of the theater, and from the rest he hears, as if they were moths eating in a nearer room, a sound of paper and wings as the lights go fully down, and it is time.

With a soft clearing of the throat, he begins.

"Now then. We shall state the thing plain…"

War Mosquitoes

THESE FILAMENT MOSQUITOES ARE TETHERED to thin cord made of silk of a thickness three molecules wide. They were once deployed at the front to stitch wounds.

The mosquitoes perform their task by struggling in and out of the wounds. They flatten their bodies, pierce, and drag the ligature behind them, fly out to the end of their thread, then loop back in. In and out, these stalwart creatures go deep inside, to the organs even, stitching. Their small but formidable, tiny barbed toes attach to the soldier and are strong enough to resist even the force of arterial bleeding that otherwise might flush them away.

Many of these insects, having lived long lives of exceptional service, made it back to the Medical Corps Tent, drawn by a pheromone. An attendant would examine their wings under a magnifier and determine their fitness for another mission. One mosquito had stitched a full ten meters of filament, according to records. Others had done nearly as much. Those who can't go on are released into an enclosure with a pond about the size of a tire. After death each was placed in its own box made of glass, little glass boxes not much bigger than a thumbnail, with magnifying lenses on the outside and pressurized with argon gas. And so here we are.

Magnified in their individual capsules, they rest eternally in the museum. One can see each in its dun-colored uniform, with specks of gold hung from the thinnest of ribbons, which are medals. It seems an absurd gesture. Until you look closer. One has a mustache. It may be painted on, or it may have grown that way. It even has some grey hairs in it. Another mosquito wears corrective lenses connected by a wire. Many of the name and rank labels have come unglued from their frames inside.

The argon gas escaped long ago. The exoskeletons are impossibly thin, made of plates like airships shot full of holes and tattered. In places you can see right through them.

.

Spawning

THE FAST-MOVING CURRENT, ABOUT THE size of a billiard table, clear and cold, holds the grayling frozen in time. The resin we look through has been carefully pulled when warm to achieve the ridges and the knife edges. The bottom stones are blue like the backs of the fish—dark blue— side by side in their slenderness, jostling. One is bent at the middle in the act of shivering up the stream, and the feeling is that this individual is fatigued…though this is likely wrong. Grayling may spawn many times, going a hundred miles sometimes, as we've come to regret in a city when the cold creeks are full of them, smelling of thyme (hence the scientific name *Thymalis arcticus*): multiple generations spawning in muscular darkness swaying in the resin as you walk past.

Michaux writes of a fishing trip he took deep in the city where, at the inlet to the black lake, deep in the woods, he slit open the grayling stomachs to find two pygmy shrews in a paste of mosquitoes, "wet and sleeping."

Pebbles go up to stones on the top shore of the creek, white stones. Red alder cones from last year hang over the water (their stems originate out of sight on the other side of the resin and mosquitoes rest upside down on the new leaves). Tyne Warblers, their orange caps light in the shadow. They had gone extinct here. During the spawning festival, in celebration of the return of the fish from their beginnings in the diorama, some people still wear a sprig of thyme over the course of the day and use it in dishes that evening.

This river picks up later, in another diorama.

The Veldt

A DIORAMA MUST HAVE AN air of falsity. It must disappoint.

We can never go inside, where everything is deeply simple. All the death that will ever be has already occurred. Michaux two centuries ago called this, "The land of the confines." This is why the viewer (in gazing through temporal distances), while complicit, is never to blame. The same cannot be said of a cleverly done zoological habitat, the kind for the tiniest of voles, say, who have no idea of their real harborage; neither is it true for the transparent lizards of the Fountain District, which were netted at the approach of the Fire and which thrive to this day in the Terrarium of the Folds. We sympathize with a creature to which we, ourselves, have done the harm.

Michaux said we desire the entrapment of the diorama. If we were to cross over, our skin would register the breezes, the merciless sunlight, the cries of the birds. That place behind the glass, where lies the Veldt, is of a tactile nature, all texture. The only—the only—unforgivable flaw in a business that makes itself perfect by deceit can be found in the joining of the background (often a curved surface, painted to the horizon) to the taxidermical preparations in the nearer ground. More on this later. To which we add the complaint that we cannot touch it.

A stag's rump, but what lies round the edge, the far edge, of the stag's rump? Nothing less than the rest of the world. The mind makes it more enchanting, knowing we cannot see what could be seen, because the totality is only out of view. As a secret just beyond our grasp, kept from us by our friends and that we know to leave alone.

Wild Dogs

TEN WILD DOGS TEAR AT the carcass of a stentor antelope. The interior has become transparent with an impossible vapor, a "smoke of blood," backed by the arches of the ribcage. Michaux has inserted a kind of gel, and made it invisible, to achieve this effect.

While off to the side two dogs fight over a choice bit of gore (likely the liver), the others of the pack are positioned around this large antelope, which, were it not prone, would stand ten feet at the shoulder. The dogs' hindquarters are lowered as for tug-of-war, jaws clamped in pulling, straining attitudes. All round, ravens watch, their bodies black sheaves. One bird, head lowered, appears to be calling. The essence of opportunity is to abstain; the raven is made of such knowledge.

But as for the dogs, two of the pack have seen human contact. This creature has a leather collar, tooled with a name just out of sight; another, a diagonal cut in the ear, indicating she has been caught, sterilized, and released. These dogs are not actual wild dogs but were purchased from a veterinary clinic for use in the museum (there had been an accident at the kennel). So the dusty, the violent life is depicted using their skins. The collar comes from elsewhere as well, from another dog that may have lived a happy, and only marginally mysterious, life in the city. Such things the diorama will coax us to forget.

The opened carcass glistens with the damp—it must have been a sudden end—and the blood as well, darkening the grasses, points to the chief success of the Wild Dog Diorama: this ability to achieve wetness by way of lacquer and lovely tricks of lighting. In the far distance, painted on the background, is the remnant of the stentor herd that, with the implacable, shoulder-to-shoulder defense of their species, stands watching the dogs, always to *mark*, to not lose sight of, the dogs' whereabouts.

In *Photographs of Dioramas*, Toyle draws a link between violence and the watching of violence and finally, of non-intervention. The photograph, in Toyle's view, is completed not at the dry click of the shutter but when it becomes a solid fact. Over time perspective becomes internal. The photograph itself need not be taken at all. Perspective occurs in the mind, floating along the glass. The choice, therefore, of a single angle from which to view the diorama, as if one had become paralyzed, is the great strength, and also the grave limitation, of all such photography.

Toyle would have us instead return to the diorama's beginnings, to the single peephole, a lens-like place, often with magnification, through which to look. We would gaze through, *look across,* as along a lane tented by black trees in which the moonlight pours over distant grasses on the other side, and see the curatorial strangeness is magnified to an almost metaphysical cast. Quaint sights, even horrors, are given the permissiveness of size. This is the Nook effect. The little living room, used to sell furniture, in some unaccountable way, resembles the scene of a murder. The separation of a scene from its surroundings creates a sense of drama, if not doom.

A killdeer, you note, upright on the dirt patch, with her three eggs in the ground nest, adds witness to the event.

An Animal

ONCE, WHEN I WAS A child, I saw a taffy-puller working away inside a candy shop. The mass of the candy—it had to weigh forty pounds—would fall, you see—or try to fall—but it could not—it could only sag—sustained by the revolving arms.

The blob of candy would gather, bulge, and be stretched. It would flash along its surface and strain, to be struck in its midsection and borne upward by the arms of the machine. In the candy I saw a person sagging at a desk hunch and vomit a new shape. I saw fingers trying to make a sign while they burned together. I saw some featherless bird try to get away, then dive into itself. The candy had entered a state of exception: here was an animal that could be formed but never known, an animal that could not get away and whose only recourse was to torture those who looked at it. Striations in the taffy like muscle stretched when cool. Rips and tears almost developed—polyp-bubbles of air—and the intolerable pinks as the woman added the food dye—into the organs or the skins, there was no telling them apart—folded into the soft glow of the shop while confectioners stood at tables cutting things up.

A spiritual secret waited there; one not for the finding but merely for the waiting, to be present, you see, to be unknown. If I had been forced to articulate the secret, I would have stammered out something like, *the only one*. The only mystery—no, this was an *experiment*, an experiment in falling. It was almost funny to watch the taffy start out in its reverie only to realize it wasn't supposed to touch the floor. And as

I watched the homunculus become purple and, as if in decay, haul itself back onto the revolving sticks, plummeting tile-ward like a circus ride in which people who had been pressed together were trying to digest their fear, it seemed like nostalgia itself, containing the conditions of growing up as well as the memory of them, and you wanted the long candy back, the paper and the wax, yet there it was right before you. It had never gone.

Meanwhile, a teardrop shape had formed in the candy gone completely mauve, with deep fissures of blue. Stretched, it reflected the shop window and showed me in my hat, elongated, before the plait of the next collision with itself—a wet smack that couldn't be heard—and buried me, the me before as a handful of liver, under a darkness a hundred thousand years lean. A single animal that had been invented at the Farmers College and had not yet *quite* come into its genetics but had been intended to fly, one day.

Curation

AND WHY HAD THEY CHOSEN these things?

Because curation too is an act of despair.

Michaux would dissect the vocal cords of birds. He would lay them out as a series of severed rings. Fresh, intact vocal cords he would attach to a little bellows which he would pump with his finger while pushing on the side walls of the throat to produce different sounds. (To keep them damp, he would give them a little spritz now and then.) And then he would draw conclusions about their songs. Michaux had a collection of these sounds saved on wax cylinders, but by his own admission the recordings were often "quite monstrous." Frog sounds, digestive in nature.

In studying the syrinxes of known bird species, Michaux was able to locate the tracheal rings in carefully sawn bird fossils as well—and to produce in the imagination a catalogue of *possible sounds* which he inferred had been among the potential melodies the birds could have uttered. In truth, he didn't believe he could really know. Reality can never overcome imagination; imagination can never overcome reality. The two live uneasily together. Much of the world's pain is because of this. And that, he noted, is as it should be.

II: H. AUGUST MICHAUX

Kaleidoscope

DOESN'T THE PROJECTOR LIGHT UP there—the sun—seem to polish the dark? It is as if a yellow cone were being turned on a lathe. We've been using the same projector—and wooden carriage—from the beginning, you know. But I was just thinking of optics in general—and their interventions. What struck me just now, before the light went out, were the flecks in the cone, which I could just see prior to their emergence (it seemed to me) into the dawn light.

When I was a boy, I would take apart my mother's kaleidoscopes. I would organize them on my tabletop. And when I was done, I would put them for the most part back together again.

I liked, especially, having made my own little omniumgatherum. The flies and worms. The cardboard and shapes. The uncanny dust, now discorporated, now broadcast and drifting, all there on the table. I thought the kaleidoscope must be the loveliest toy that has ever been. The carousels always turned, as if oozing, into someone else's thoughts. I felt they were sentient when broken up, subject to self-knowledge in a way they could never be when integrated. Long bones of cardboard and wood, of tongue depressors and such, glued, the kaleidoscopes had too many analogies that I imagined were painful to them. Why they were always hidden for some other purpose—not nefarious, mind you—but so *other* that the parts could only wait to become whole again, knowing they lived uneasily next to one another in association. These things have a way of becoming…

There were surprisingly few things inside the kaleidoscopes. They were all roughly the same: the Trope of the Five Mirrors. These mirrors, numbered for no reason I could discern, gave the splitting affect, and the bulb at the far end rolling wetly loose as if to imitate in glass some essential feature of the human eye—a sort of oil capsule with the shards inside I would turn this way and that against the light. The oil must be the proper viscosity, you know. I learned this when I left one near an open window in the fall. On a cold day the kaleidoscope is slow, in sympathy with the cold. Time behaves again. There may still be time. To see them move. For the moist carnival.

Interestingly, you could put a magnet against the ball of a certain kaleidoscope, and by some magnetic resonance or other, pull the shards with iron in them, thin as flakes from some decaying bridge, and bulge the entire view—so that, even though you were separate, you had some control, somewhat, as to what would happen inside. But as for the cold, the shards mark out their passage almost casually, in that gelid oil, like tumbling cities from afar. But warm them, and they move with an essential logic. Glass and pieces of carriages and hidden machine-springs flex their guts into all manner of disappearances. You can't track or trace the same shard, and furthermore, made of glass and other see-through things, the shards are forever lensing one another in phantom, extrawindow leavings, always parting ways or being destroyed in the next intersection of the lines, which naturally are the seams of the Trope of the Five Mirrors.

I had read somewhere that some flies can sense magnetic fields and use them to navigate and that the sensor allowing this lies deep inside them: a simulacrum of a world structure deep inside their singularity. Indeed, it is as if you're looking into the mind of a fly when you look through a kaleidoscope.

Kaleidoscope II

WHEN THE KALEIDOSCOPES WERE WHOLE again, I didn't like to look through them for very long. I don't know what person could. Certainly, my mother never could. Kaleidoscopes boil the world. But they do so as if to render an animal high in a ritual under a roof of slate. I would peek through them, then, to ratify something. And that was all. To this day I don't like them, and really I do believe my mother didn't like them, either. They were talismans to her, a past pain or unhappiness. On my mother's passing I received the little cases in which she kept them, and while I left their lids closed and on a shelf somewhere, I did hold onto them. I found they exerted an influence, like sound over distances. I felt compassion for them.

This is no toy. The inside of this animal, this kaleidoscope, is a diorama by way of its hidden plan, as if both the structure and the kaleidoscope must never become immobile, lest they become a picture.

There is a saying about dioramas the origin of which is difficult to pin down. The story goes that when you look at a diorama, you must never look behind you—where another diorama is sure to be—lest the scene in front of you disappear and you become responsible for its destruction…

We should mention that Michaux held to this notion of "archeological taxidermy." He came to this orientation (and Mary Retherford was to take it from here, much later) by way of the things in the old sites that came out of the ground. He wished to clothe them. "To clothe" was the verb he used, for he believed that the aim of taxidermy was to garment the specimen "in the raiment of its own soul again." That the skin was the soul seems to have been implied here. Or, at the very least, the skin's relationship to the soul, turning in the cone of light. Can you feel it? Did Michaux feel it? There's no evidence whatsoever.

Yet one *can*.

Michaux

In his second term at school, Michaux found taxidermy. "I was drawn to the stillness," he writes. "And to the silence." Dioramas seemed the perfect medium for the expression of life. "All was there, nothing was left out. I spent all of my time in the museum. I began to see the whole world there." Once, while on term break, when the school had closed the labs and there was no excuse to stay, he went alone on a trout fishing expedition. The chosen stream, which he doesn't name, passed through the ruins of an ancient parking structure, a library and shops glistening on the banks where the bricks were swept smooth. In a series of pools formed by beaver dams he chanced upon a rare, greenback cutthroat trout, which he caught with a caddis fly. With unusual intensity he describes the scallops on the gills, "scallops of death," of the small, firm fish in the palm of his hand. He releases that cold creature, mysterious as an atavism, back into the stream. It begins to rain. It rains for two days. The creek is too swift for fishing. His expedition ends. The *Journal*, too, ends here. It doesn't resume till a year and two months later. But the truth is some change came over Michaux during the course of that journey. Afterward, he seems to have gone into another room in himself, a room requiring not words but thoughts.

In the resumption of the *Journal* we find a Michaux more mature, and focused. He begins to isolate himself in his room, reading the accounts of Teggetmeier, Corbett, Smithe the Elder, and others on the animals that had once been there and whose mechanical twins still roamed the groves of ailanthus and buckthorn, box elder, yew and honeysuckle, sycamore maple, black locust and jack pine, threaded through one another below the unusual city sky. He alternated his now-graduate studies with continued solo expeditions into the forest, going in search of these animals and insects—and if he couldn't find them, inventing them—and putting them in dioramas, a medium in which he soon surpassed his teachers.

"Dioramas do not depict the seen (the species, the environs), but the unseen. The animal before you is thus the least important part of the game."

Basements

As a boy, I liked that he'd had himself put in a diorama. When I was young, I would go and see him in his office. Something morbid in me was drawn to that encapsulation, the museum-like trappings in the window. I felt he was alive. The next moment, I understood he wasn't. This flipping of awareness would go back and forth. Just when I had a handle on it, the feeling would flip back: there the man is. The great man himself. And then he would be gone, having never moved from his place, affable at his desk. I found this intoxicating until one day they removed the diorama. And in fact most of these dioramas are in storage now. Michaux's diorama is no exception.

Michaux's Office

IN FACT, MICHAUX WAS THE very first instance of a person, an actual person, appearing by consent in a diorama. Or, at least, so went the mythology, and thus Michaux popularized the practice of *Voluntary Entry* into the diorama. He insisted on this in his will, and due to his prominence the thing went forward. So when he died, the office he'd occupied at the museum was packed up, piece by piece, to the museum's new wing, the morning gleam of his early risership down-glancing from high windows onto the carpets (an affect done with gelled lights).

A fire, sculpted of glass thin as smoke, burned in the grate. He had a globe he was painting. There was a papier-mâché ball. The box of colors lay open. He had paused, with the void gleam of all dioramic figures, to look at me. He seemed to smile, to be not pleased but tolerant, as if I were a servant come in with the tea caddy.

I liked that he had a little broken-down cat, called Jones, curled up geriatrically in a chair facing the fire, and that he had rolled that chair near to warm her. In all his biographical sketches, however, I never found reference to a cat. Later, I would worry that the cat wasn't real, was a sort of visual reference to Michaux's field of study.

I wanted to sit with him, to hear his voice, to know with my own hand about the problem of Jones, whether she were real and would accept me, accept my touch, and start up her engine. I fancied that the small talk between Michaux and myself would begin there, with that fishbone of a jaw-stroke and the somber engine of the cat. My, but

Michaux would have despised such sentimentality. And I must say, that cat, though her surface had buckled inward somewhat, humanized the man. He gained by her presence that which, in her, had been caused to be human. The affect may have been intentional.

Minister Goll visited the Michaux diorama as well. The few letters of Goll's that have survived tell of a sundial in that office. Minutes on end, Goll says, he spent looking into that golden library. Only, there never was a sundial in Michaux's office. Goll must have imagined it there. Or he had it removed.

"How nothing that has gone will ever be gone forever." The surrogate looms.

Memory

SLIDE PLEASE, JEFFREY.

Do you remember?

Teasel

FOR SEVERAL MONTHS, I WOULD go again and again with my museum pass and peer into his office. The personality of a room will give us the room's code. The teasel in the jar. The fray at the corner of the chair, right down to the horsehair's black oil flung out like insect antennae, as if that chair were a cocoon just now prickling into the office a black shape. The first black shape.

Michaux meant for rooms to be read. There were rules. Grammars. Structure. The near rooms, even their presence, told of that chair off to the left, used as a visual reference (the teasel in the jar to the carding teasel and its use in the wool industry in which his family made its fortune). If we lacked the journal in which Michaux planned this room, we would never have known. As things stand, we don't know why he took the trouble. Every room is full of pain. Why add more?

But also how light, pulled from the windows, gives responsibility to the desk lamp for the Nook Effect at night (the light changes again, at 1-to-4800 scale, night coming quickly, the fire glowing more redly), suffuses glass jewels, cabinets. Reflections in the glass of a second cabinet unfurl pale blooms of tumblers at certain hours, a set of bird skulls, pestles, mortars. How all objects, especially knobs, are polished by the oncoming dark.

Weekly Pigeon Loft Report

I NOW LIVE IN A retirement block for museum personnel. I have recently moved here. Of eight planned lectures, I made it to five. Now, I lecture in my mind.

Nothing to be done.

Thomas is my neighbor. We have both been forcibly retired by the Department of Dioramas, me just a month ago and Tom some months before that. Our balconies are conjoined, separated by a rail. It is evening. We look down into the street where the dust is settling, as by static electricity, over the golden concatenated windows of the shops, which all have gone reflective.

Tom had been a museum accountant. Now, he monitors numbers and number-like things. He pays special attention to the weekly Pigeon Loft Report in the newspapers, an often-long list of the band numbers of pigeons that have gotten lost in flight and either gone missing (M), died (D), or turned up in another loft (X, for "crossed over"). These numbers he uses to direct his Mote predictions and to play the lottery.

Some birds are found a hundred miles or more from their point of origin; in such cases the distance traveled will be appended to the X code. The pigeons of different government agencies, as well as the birds of private citizens, and wild birds that have been banded and released make up the total. Tom's affinity for numbers causes him to search for patterns, which he has been entering into charts over the months and years. He has discovered that the band numbers repeat on a seven-year cycle—the same pigeons getting lost, dying, or crossing into different lofts, over and over again. He shows me the evidence, complete with news clippings he keeps in a ledger. We sit in silence while the moths drift in and out of the vines.

He is convincing. I feel he is on to something. The last birds are going quiet out there.

"They're caught in time, Wiggins," he says to me.

Apartment Block

I HAVE FOUR ROOMS I'M still getting used to. I have a guest room, a small kitchen, and a combination living room/den/library looking out onto the balcony. I sleep in my office, which is also a rather large closet. The complex is new and almost entirely empty. People—an entire generation nearing retirement—move in every week. It is early summer.

Previously, I lived in another building in another part of the city.

I eat out of cans—elegant cans, their tops etched—due to the time savings and the incredibly high quality and standard of the foods of the canned goods industry. I like grayling in oil. I like pigeon in tomato sauce. But my favorite is probably—

It doesn't matter.

(Well, Dolgo crabapple is probably my favorite. It is the crabapple closest in spirit to the apple.)

The guest room has stayed empty, except for shelves and a bare floor and a bed. When the sun touches the bed, the room smells of linen. It's where I keep the dioramas I'm working on. Usually, when I am finished with a diorama—I've made two so far—I place it on the bed, not the shelves.

Being Begin

I LIKE TO KEEP MY hand in. Tom does, too. We exchange theories—quietly, as if we are the only ones who thought these things—I about Michaux's Diorama Numbering System (MDNS), and he about the radio and phone systems and packet-switching: how a message, a voice or a set of codes for a document, is split into pieces and sent over the lines in different directions, taking different routes, to be reassembled at the end as a sound or a message. Tom says that these pieces got *stranded* sometimes and never coalesced again and were still in the lines, forming a whole that would never be joined. And finally, that a message—a call, a voice—would be sent over the lines more than once, in stutters, and in the inevitable event of a piece (of the whole) being lost, it could still be reassembled at the other end, like the new leaves of the corpse verbena, *Verbena chaemocadiveris.*

But these messages, he says, break up at the approaches to the Number. He said that word, "number," with a keen emphasis, as if it were larger than a regular number, as if it made up what the phones were saying to themselves about themselves.

Portrait

A GENERATION AGO, EVERY SCHOOLCHILD was familiar with Michaux. Most of us, along about grade four, would have been instructed to bring a shoebox to school. I've been told that even today this is done. Do you remember? We stood the shoebox on its side with the top removed, thus creating the nook, the little niche. And in that place we glued a backdrop which we had painstakingly drawn. We cut our animals out of cardstock, and in they went, into the created world. As children we were taught that Michaux, too, liked animals. He wanted to preserve something of their strangeness. He wanted to give them a place to live, a habitat for that essential thing about them. Our shoebox dioramas were displayed in one way or another and a little competition (as to the best one) set up, judged by the ancient librarian. They showed us slides of strange animals in different poses.

So we remember having studied Michaux, and that is all, on the way toward a more robust science than could be found in taxidermy. But the diorama is uniquely suited to children, and it seems to me there is something quite childlike about Michaux.

Michaux was obsessed with environments. He helped others, gave them money. He was a kind of saint for whom ethics was a chief concern. He wanted to know how this process of taxidermy, and of science in general, could go forward in a kindly manner.

There is also the distant and isolated Michaux whom colleagues described variously as a scholar, a philosopher, and an obsessive. There was a sloppiness to the rest of his life, as his *Journals* clearly show.

He was a man of dice. And the coining of birds. When his mother passed away, he abandoned domestic life altogether. He set up a cot in his office—an experimental bedroom—and his journals record the epiphany that he needn't sleep anywhere else. The museum had all he needed by way of companionship. So he made his home there.

Michaux was one of our Great Walkers. He walked as many as fifteen miles a day over the ruins of the city, "half forest, half train compartment," as he rather famously described the confinement of the woods and their decaying rooms. He wore through countless shoes, and he saved them all in a closet, curled up in a pile like animals that had been shot. Mary Retherford, the great dioramist of her day, considered making a display of her predecessor's shoes but ended up changing course.

Michaux was a committed vegetarian and Mote enthusiast. He records with grim humor his many Mote losses. The pliant wisps of this, our national game, challenged him endlessly. He stayed up half the night going over his wagers and predictions, and the cries of the wild dogs reached him through the open window—and crickets and other night sounds particular to his time and still present in our own.

Michaux's eccentricities were tolerated. This was often the case then. In times of great wealth and inexhaustible resources, obsessions become total. Strangely for a man who believed in the human project of the museum, he seems not to have had many friends. He believed beauty and learning were the museum's chief aims, and they were to be found inside oneself. His *Journals* indicate that he may have had one romance, but given his reticence on the subject (and the difficulty of separating the mythology—that alcove of comfort—from what really occurred), we can't be sure how far the thing went.

At any rate, any complexity appertaining to the life of Michaux was internal to that man. There is no separating the man of the Nook (and its effects) from the person who lived and breathed in the city. I honestly don't know if I'd want to. We have to maintain the Nook, while holding on, if we can, to a certain skepticism. We would do better to focus on the work, I should think. Put the shoebox to proper use, you know.

Tom

TOM OFTEN SITS ON THE balcony, elbows on knees, head hung down, presiding over a large stomach. His eyes are open, fixed on some object just at the edge of the balcony, a half smile on his lips. On a balcony opposite, wind roses turn hectically in pots. The geese are flying. Tom and I watch them in their long Vs vanish behind chimneys and reappear and vanish till they are lost in the somewhere, out near the First Seventh Bank, on 7,475th Street. The sun strikes the trees as an orange powder.

Tom wears slippers, his shirt never tucked. A telephone on the side table. When the phone rings, he lifts the receiver and listens. After a moment, with a diagnostic posture of the head, he speaks. He says he's listening to the clicks on the line, like coins far within a vending machine, listening to the packets switching, then coalescing, in the earpiece. I am surprised that he's maintained his calm, quiet rationality.

"I don't watch the street too closely anymore," he says. "Too many patterns."

The Empty Diorama

Now then. The glacier's border, like a surface of white dice and curtains, tumbles megafauna out of its mouth every so often. City things, too: the innards of the past, which turn out to be ordinary, spill out of its white furnace. This is an image I have always associated with Michaux because he loved dice and collected them. Metal, ivory, wood, he didn't care—resin—even little dice made from teeth. These last he kept in a drinking glass. Slide, Jeffrey.

A glacier is violence held in check. Its time stamp is similar to that of the diorama. The three or four glaciers that remain in the city give us a faint startle and a *reset* of what it once meant to Be, in "the annihilatory condition before Being." The gunk of the before times thaws uneasily. Such as this group of travelers who got snowed in in the high country. They are just emerging, like goods made of leather, from the shelves of dice. And this house plant, blackened by ice but still identifiable as the split-leaf philodendron, must have been dear to someone to have been taken on such a journey. And this boy's bird cage, with its purple finches stuck to the droppings at the bottom, all leathern, as if they'd forgotten to suffer and have simply resigned themselves to become useful to the snow. Things tumbling out of the great safe of the glacier, returning to us an apprehension of secrecy. The glacier, like the diorama, is a mechanism of storage (but not always retrieval).

Horticultural Mandate

ABOUT THIS SAME PERIOD, AGED nine—the time of the kaleidoscopes—I
kept a pet fly. You had to go into a lottery and be chosen. This was to
teach us children our responsibility to the Horticultural Mandate. It
was a yellow-tufted fly (*Musca domestica tenuem*), the kind with a fine
yellow feather on the top of its head—that it raises up and down like a
crest—if you've seen them.

You set up a jar, and you gave the fly a dish of water and piece
of fruit, a decayed chunk of apple as I recall, red-green as if it had
been gouged out of the sun. The fly would sit there and eat. Then
have a wash. We were told that while all individual flies are unique,
we mustn't name them, because it would be difficult to let them go.
I held assiduously to this rule. A bit later, you put in a cube of meat.
I did everything according to instructions. And she would fly around
the jar. At the proper time I released the fly into my part of the
city. The open window I remember distinctly. She was there, at its
edge. Then all at once, she winked out, disappearing over the hedge.
Not long after, the young flies began to hatch in the jar. I watched
the little maggots crawl and struggle on the meat. When they were
grown, I let them go, too. Clean, sleek flies, with the business of the
world in mind. They vanished in that same way over the hedge. (I
remember they were installing a pipe in the road all that summer.)
I sent my count and my report to the government and did a small
presentation to my class at school. I thought I'd get another fly, but I

wasn't selected again. There were too many boys and girls. There is a relationship between flies and kaleidoscopes. But I suppose in some small way I did my part.

Michaux Diorama Numbering System

As I say, Michaux designed a numbering system for dioramas, known
as the Michaux Diorama Numbering System (MDNS), based on the
coordinate systems for nautical and land maps. But unlike the standard
grid corresponding to fixed places on the earth and the map, Michaux's
dioramas were scattered in the different museums of the city. Distinct
as well from the museum's own, multivalent classing, descriptive and
subject-based systems, which direct the scholar to the location of each
display on, say, manta rays (of which there are thirty-two), even if the
displays are far from one another in space and time, Michaux first
positioned dioramas far in advance of their actual creation, in a grid.

At first, the grid bore an X and a Y axis, and the alphanumeric
coordinates, represented as single squares, were of a standard size. So,
a diorama may fetch up at T32 or F09 and so forth. But as we've seen,
dioramas vary wildly in size and shape. Because of this, more than
one diorama might share the available space in a given grid square,
labeled N, S, E, W, to indicate where on the square it would go. Each
of the quadrants of a square might also be split into quadrants—for
the smallest of the dioramas—and this problem Michaux solved by
attaching a number, up to sixteen were possible, for each sixteenth of
an original square: so a small diorama might bear the alpha-numeric
superscript, $T^{183}N^8$, to designate the 8th square of the North Quadrant
of the 183rd square in the T region of the grid.

But Michaux was not satisfied with this system.

What would happen, for example, if a diorama were destroyed?

Presence

WE ARE AN AGENT, IN part, of extinction. "As the bee builds a musculature of wax unique to itself," we build both the concept of extinction and its physical reality in the form of cells of absence, "made of ideation." We build extinction itself as a concrete reality. We assemble absence as part of who we are. We give the extinguished an actual shape, and we call it memory, and we build, as well, the shadow-building beside it, the analysis of extinguishment. That is our most fundamental trait. It is really quite sudden, that architecture all around us, as love.

We are an agent of return. This was Michaux's most fundamental belief.

And so in this empty diorama, depicting preservation strategies, the elk have been removed from their meadow. Note the silence particular to absence. We see their footprints: where the gravel application ends, the hooves would go. In a tableau designed for a herd in particular, the surrounding details recede. Without them, the room, which has been designed for them, has no reason for being.

The elk are undergoing mite treatment, which is a simple process of combing the powder, which has been dyed to match their coats, into the hairs. The informational silhouette-and-key tell us there were six, one a calf. There is a distant shape to their departure, yet everything remains the same. The willow stems the same length where they've been nipped, the cloud high and bright. The river appears to move.

Did Michaux foresee the return of these creatures taken from dioramas? Though he may have wished it, my sense is, in new circumstances, were he alive today, he would have sought a new "negative shape," a new present-absence, to account for these living creatures and their return. In his time many of the animals of the city were mechanical. Michaux would see the stoaten herd, whose members lumber in the city's forests, never startle. They have no fear at loud sounds, at the bustle of trams. Instead, they chew circularly, their noses drifting up into the trees to drip gobbets of chlorophyll onto the pavements. Michaux would say it is we who are absent to them and as such would make reference to our shadows, like worsted assistants, carrying our bags and things at the wrong angle and flustered to keep up, even when they precede us.

Return

EFFORTS TO INSTILL FEAR INTO the herds of the city are of note. Fear, that "necessary condition of wildness." They have fenced Ward Four and set loose predators, at first wolves (who prefer deer and whom were of little use) and then wild dogs, whom it seems would kill anything, and did. These dogs attacked several stoaten in full view of the herd. The animals' cries, their blatting in surprise at the novelty of pain (for they were unable to understand what was happening), communicated to the others, to the "witnesses," and two of the twelve who knew no fear were "converted" on the instant. They were given that necessary gift back. After several weeks, those that remained followed suit. But the stoaten remained unbothered and unterrified of ourselves. Even our four-legged companions on leash in the bright morning fogs with the sound of their canine nails on the sidewalk, so pert and interested, didn't bother them.

Michaux would say that for the stoaten we are the "emptiness's capacitance." He liked such phrases. The purpler, the better.

Michaux Diorama Numbering System II

AFTER TWENTY YEARS, MICHAUX REPLACED his Diorama Numbering System. About this time, we notice the appearance of another set of numbers on the tops and the bottoms of the dioramas. We see that he added letters, U and D, for "up" and "down." Thus, on older dioramas you find a black line through the old code and the new code placed next to it. This is because Michaux had moved into three dimensions—for dioramas in caves, in the canopy, or the sky—and away from "a blank chorology."

He reasoned that to locate something in three-dimensional space, you need as reference surfaces at least two other dioramas. So dioramas in the new system will have their own coordinates scribed on the back, in the center, and the codes of the adjacent dioramas on each of the five sides.

But what if one or both of the reference dioramas had not been created yet? As evidenced by long lists of numbers and subject matter of dioramas that had never been made, Michaux gave a number to dioramas that he wished to make, but hadn't yet done.

The new numbering system has a curious feature: the numbers on the back of dioramas grow outward from a point of origin: a reference diorama, the number 0,0,0, buried in the center. This number never appears on any diorama, but it is possible to find. I must find it.

Forest $^{303}T79W^{04}$

AT THE SOUTH ENTRANCE OF the museum stood the forest diorama in the city's largest Wardian case, or terrarium, plate glass in a wood frame, sealed with wax, towering overhead. And there you could observe through the plate at different levels of mezzanine a great variety of forest life. Unlike most dioramas, this is a wholly mechanical forest filled with creatures most of which are animatronic in some capacity. Even the leaves move as if in a dying wind. Yet below, all is stillness in the ferns, at first. In Michaux's time, a version of this case would have stood on a desktop and produced its own rain.

Mechanical forest creatures move in the bower and sunlight. The "sun" tracks back and forth at 1:4800 scale, giving the impression of a frenetic business in the interior spaces.

At times, to simulate dusk or dawn, the inward privacy of a red light pours into the case from somewhere within. Mechanical mosquitoes and other insects cloud the inner world. Wind-up voles creep into the open and flit out of sight. Legions of mice cross the ground in a flurry of industrial activity. We can see one carrying a simulated seed toward here, where there is a pile of them. He deposits the seed and returns for another.

Ants single file their way up a Thenders fir, done in plaster. Up they go, up the trunk, and if you look closely, you can see the track they run in. In this extreme close-up they disappear over the top of a crotch and reappear below. Two of the ants are missing a fleck of paint, the only indication of their artificial nature, save perhaps the too-straight track-like trail they follow.

But otherwise, even their little legs move.

Coining

IN A TRIANGULAR CASE AT the join of two hallways, a grackle lies on its side on a bit of green. The half-round of a trash bin frames the right side (done in papier-mâché). A wrapper with torn lettuce, the seed of a pickle in the cracked white. The bird's eye is closed. The lid is of a lighter hue than the black of its feathers. No iridescence flows over the body at present, for the back of the bird, where the mirrors—shafts, really—of the iridescence reside, faces partly down, tipped away, the two legs gathered in, in an almost flinching gesture.

A single coin, a penny, rests on the upper breast in the join of the wing (which is also folded). The whole scene is bright, as if it were midafternoon. Perhaps lunch has ended, and there has been a rush back to the offices, away from the bench whose leg bends into view on the right-hand side.

And now, everyone has gone, and the park abides. Age. Disease. We don't know, really. The penny gleams.

Someone has coined this bird. To coin a bird is to tie oneself to it. To fashion it as an allotment. To also (and this is the deeper part) call to other birds, to the ones in the umbrella's fragile elbows and whom are watching out of sight. To reach, through the coin, to another region.

Michaux was a great coiner, you know. His *Journals* are full of specific instances. Penny on crow. Something seemed to have been at it, unquote. Pigeon near D Station. Birds carry the awareness of the twin world.

Each got a penny. He liked green pennies the best. Their plantlike way, as if the man in profile were underwater. I once did a little survey of the *Journal* and discovered three hundred and eighty-four references to specific birds. I published a small paper on it that I'm not unproud of. I do not know what to make of it, coining. The practice has power in spite of itself.

Also there are two little mites, little glassy beads, on the grackle. Are they coming to stay, or are they going? Do they abandon at the flight of temperature their "iridescent ride"?

The beak is partly open, and the tongue can just be seen.

Neighbor

CARLA HAS MOVED IN AROUND the corner. Standing at the railing and leaning, I see a spotted leg in a house dress, the shin bone shining. She recrosses her ankle and coughs. When I say hello, there is a pause. Then a head full of curly hair appears and a hand fits glasses in place. A small dog comes into view and sits, tipping its head.

Carla had been retired only three weeks before. She had been a traditional woodworker hired to do up rooms in the Town using the tools and methods of previous centuries, to achieve the authenticity necessary to farmhouses and cottages. She had made furniture for the dens and libraries of middle-class homes as well, where subtle tool marks, left there on purpose, had to be to period. She also added these features, such as plane chatter marks, onto furniture that had been made in factories. Over the years she had become an expert in the weathering of window frames and doors, aging them differently on what the dioramists meant to be the windward sides of buildings. Someone else would come behind her to add moss, or lichen, depending on the climate. Carla had reached master level two decades ago. She trained an entire generation of craftswomen, who have since replaced her.

Her hands are quite young, and strong. She opens jars for me. I have heard that one of the ways to prevent the pain of arthritis is to keep active. But this is also one of the ways to cause arthritis.

Freedom

CARLA DYES HER HAIR BLACK and wears it loose, in a cloud. She is small and compact and stands with her legs planted, as if in challenge. She had a husband she adored who died quite young, when they were still in love. They shared a passion for woodworking and would even get permits to reclaim blowdowns in the lots of the city, using ropes and horses and so forth. They never had children. In that sense Carla is free.

Carla has set up a place to work in the building's workshop. A massive workbench with a slab top, a crochet, and leg and tail vises. I sit on a stool. She is boring a hole through a plank with a brace and bit. She is telling me that dioramists are often difficult people.

"Snobs," she says, knifing a mark, a pencil in her teeth. "Think they own the world."

She knows things. There is an entire land inside her mind.

When I pepper her with questions about the Diorama of the Town—what is it really like there, and so forth, what did she really do on a daily basis and in what region of that vast space—Carla compresses her lips, lifting her chin and giving a small, private smile that doesn't touch her eyes. I imagine the entire Town forming behind that privacy, behind the everyday. She doesn't realize what she knows how to do. Or she dismisses it, I suppose. But then again, I'm a generalist. A hermeneutician. I can't seem to leave it behind.

Luck

I HAVE WONDERED RECENTLY IF my choice to take the theen finch home—and put it in a diorama rather than to coin it—is the reason for things being as they are.

Dioramic Space

MICHAUX BELIEVED IN THE CREATION of a second and even a third diorama out of sight of the viewer. He called this phenomenon "the alchemy," to signify that which was beyond normal sense perception (though he did not name the agent, or the instrument by which it occurs).

Michaux pointed to these scenes as "familial spaces," as if they were rooms of a related but separate house where each bides its time in a stasis that we can feel under certain circumstances. The third diorama, he claims, is made "of cognition." In this state the creatures within are alive. They exist in the suspension of their faculties and motion. They are given life, actual life, at deep scale. In the Smithe-Michaux Model, dioramic time is measured at one to one hundred million relative to the passage of time in the outside world (this is obviously distinct from the aforementioned "time affects," which merely bring the artificial passage of time into the scene). Thus, for every hour that passes in the diorama one million hours pass in the outside world. Millions and millions of years pass in the outside world, but the diorama appears unchanged.

Let this soak in a moment. Dioramas exist in slow time and they contain actual life at a certain scale.

Is he mad?

Michaux thought the thaumatrope was a useful theoretical model. These extra dioramas, bewailing nothing, dwell as we do, on the other side of the image. The folding of space (accomplished at the turn of an image card), placing the veldt and the lion, the glass tank and the salamander together—but only conceptually—though they (creature and place) are just the finest of tissues apart with the eye as the subtle conjoiner, occurs in time speeded up. The image card flutters like the wing of a bird. But here, it seems to me, Michaux commits an error. Using as he does the common materials of the diorama, thing and display, place and context, as a metaphor to suggest something else entirely which is occurring outside the diorama, is to confuse perception and reality. Nothing stays in its container, ever, he seems to say.

Seth

SETH, TWO FLOORS DOWN, HAD been a cleaner of dioramas, a job one step below a conservator. In the Diorama of the Town, where he'd worked his whole life, he'd specialized in cleaning without a trace. The insides of windows, the surfaces of the animals' eyes, which would gather lint due to some sort of ionization problem—something to do with static. Seth is a slight, stooped old man, with boylike shoulders and sandy hair. His pants are too large for him, and his seat appears flat, and the pants cuffs crumple down near the floor. His house sweater is so old that it has stretched nearly to his knees, as if he'd gotten these garments from an older brother, now deceased. Seth would set his stepstools up, placing the legs carefully on the ground of a diorama, and climb up to the different specimens, then with hands pink and small, the nails cut straight and dry, he would erase any evidence of the floor protectors ever having been there as he retreated back through the hidden doors.

I ask him why the lint gets in.

"It's spontaneous," he says, pushing his glasses up with a finger and pursing his lips. He has a strange habit. He licks the lenses of his glasses before cleaning them. I've also seen him place the lenses between his lips and draw them out. Then he polishes them with a cloth, all while staring in front of himself, as a person would do when alone.

We go on walks in the afternoon. Pollen from the giant chestnut trees, smelling rather disturbingly of men, collects on the new leaves, the benches, the puddle surfaces. He directs his glasses over park benches. He tells me he is making calculations—the word is his—as to whether, were he in the Town, he would clean all the pollen off, or leave it on, just to be safe. In the Diorama of the Town, he explains, he would examine pollen grains under a pocket microscope to determine which grains of pollen belong and which don't. I ask him if it were possible for pollen to be *implied* without ever being really present, and at my words Seth suddenly stops, squinting up at me, eyes keen and squeezed.

Ether flowers travel across the park.

"Are you making fun of me?" he says, his fists clenched.

I tell him of course I'm not.

Thought Problems

"GLIMPSES INTO DICE GAMES," MICHAUX wrote after a night of monitoring the game of Mote over the ticker tape, "are the most frightening. The green felt. No figure ever seems to cast but always has just done so or is about to. The opulent wristwatches, the look in their eyes. One must stand well back in order to sense here is a game of dice within the rubric of which some monumental danger is about to speak its name. We glimpse the third tower again, that stand-in for all things of a future-cast. But what, I ask, fails to have a future-cast?"

And further on: "The bell tolls a second echo especially for the person placed at the corner of sound. The liquid reflects the tower's image. I have the green stain of the bell at the corners of my mouth. And I shall help you accept. The tower exists. The dice exist. Only the man is unreal.'"

Party

SEVERAL YEARS AGO, OUR DEPARTMENT head organized an end-of-year party. The gathering was in his sumptuous home, and he hired an actor to come and play Michaux, since the anniversary of Michaux's death fell near the end of the fiscal year, and this is the kind of thing museum personnel do to amuse ourselves.

The actor, of average height, arrived in the likeness of the great dioramist at mid-career, complete with face makeup, mustache, tweed, and rugged hiking shoes. I was pleased to note that there were even burrs clinging to the bottom of a pantleg, as if he'd just come from one of his walks. Michaux held a tumbler, and that night I watched him step, with exaggerated posture, among the guests gathered round the tea or stranded in the bay windows of the drawing room—diminutive bureaucrats and technicalists all, in our sweaters and glasses, who embraced the ruse, plying Michaux with wine, which he accepted with grace, and then discreetly placed on a table somewhere. He projected—I can't deny it—a certain virility.

They engaged him in conversation.

At a distance the actor never wavered. He had that professional aloofness, necessary to gatherings of this kind, where he pretended to be kind, interested, and a little skeptical of what was said but perfectly willing to accept the possibility of saying it. The man had done his research, I'll give him that.

Someone, I forget who, kept trying to talk to me, but I heard myself replying in general terms, and soon she left me. I wanted to get home, for I had a long day ahead. I was preparing a paper on the history of the chemistry of glues that would go under review. But for some reason I couldn't leave.

Once, Michaux and I locked eyes from across the room. He seemed to be deciding whether to know me and whether to cross to where I stood. But whatever he saw in me made him turn toward the nearest guest, a rather handsome man with a great lock of hair, sure to rise in the department, and engage him in conversation.

As I watched, the two men stood before a painting of a waterfall, rocks speckled in green birds, motioning with their hands while a third guest nodded. Then later, Michaux removed a volume from the shelves and was passing it, open to a map, to another guest. All the while maintaining a benevolent detachment and calm. I felt it. We all felt it. It wasn't long before a part of me believed in who he was. He had intimate knowledge inside him. He alone knew what he had been doing all those years.

When I finally found the courage to corner him, the night was nearly over. Here and there, groups were decoalescing in a general movement toward the anteroom. I fixed him in place, his back to the bookcases. There were lines under his eyes. I remember leaning forward, gesturing, asking him about the *diorama seriatim* and how its pattern related to the numbering system he'd abandoned. I quoted him his own words: "A certain diorama may float in blackness. Or may take the shadow cast by another."

I told him what I thought he had meant. I anticipated what he would say and had follow-up questions at the ready. And as I talked— listening to myself through him—I saw behind his persona a kind of startle. His eyes grew large, as if in a panic. He was sweating, I saw. At first, he tried to improvise a response, but it soon became clear he knew nothing, could say nothing. And finally, I asked him about Goll. Hadn't he known? Shouldn't he have been able to anticipate, a hundred years into the future, what Goll would do with his, Michaux's, ideas?

At last he broke. He smiled an apology, but it was his own smile, his own apology. He seemed to plead with me. Hidden in his eyes was a shape, coming into being out of the pale grey depths, moving across the surface.

As I left the party I met a strange man, corpulent, sweating, a true friend to whiskey, with an apologetic expression coming up the entry stairs. It was a second actor, meant to play Minister Goll.

But he'd mistaken the time.

Elevator

On the day I returned to Michaux, I rode the elevator down. The collection runs into the hundreds of thousands, approaching one million. The actual number is tricky, because there are so many cataloguing systems in competition with one another, going simultaneously.

When you go down, you meet an attendant at a little elevator adjoining the lobby. You ride that barbarous conveyance of brass, known as a birdcage, down. The shaft whispers. Your heart beats. The intervening basements containing the labs—B1, B2, B3—disappear above you. Then all at once the shaft ends, becoming a metal scaffold you can look through. And through the cage, a great floor opens out, broad and flat, of Storage Basement One. It seems miles wide. And all the exhibits in rows, like tiny boxes that grow large as you approach.

When we touched down, the dioramas were like walls of differing heights floating dark on their massive pallets (sometimes covered in canvas but more often not, since all displays, taken out of the museum whole, are already sealed). There was a wooden person, a woman in a black dress, rolling one of the moving machines under one of the pallets, then pumping the handle to lift the diorama up and pull it out into the aisle—and slow, creaking, going away on down the line. The rubber wheels thumped in the cracks between stones. You could feel the great weight, at once a lightness, communicated through the floor.

That's what you leave behind when you go back up. Had it not been my job, I would have thought nothing of them, save perhaps a vague notion of their potential gathered down there. But now, I felt them. I felt all of them, out and out, level on level, in their quiet: the thousands of average—I suppose you'd say "failed"—dioramas looming like enclosed suites in the black meringue, and the freight elevator, as large as a building, bringing down still more that have been removed from the museum to make room for those sparkling, disturbing, those brilliant and perfect scenes—total scenes, clean and bright—which are continually replacing them.

Then the little birdcage elevator jerks. Someone has called it. You turn and watch the cage grow smaller and disappear into the ceiling.

Files

THE CATALOGUE CARDS COULDN'T DO them justice. They couldn't build the dioramas again in the mind, so dry the words were. (22FT x 34FT x 22FT) FOREST UNDERSTORY—SQUIRRELS—SOCIAL ASPECTS) can in no way explain that history of a way of seeing. Note the incredible size of the freight elevator. My helper stands to the side for scale. He is almost six and a half feet tall, but he looks like a figure in a train set.

My fingers walked over the tops of the cards in their drawers. And in the distance in the blank glass there must have been a backlight, because you could see the bubbles, like suspended dust. At the edges of a near display a mysterious swirl of things—like clothing, which I took to be tree limbs—and in the join of two panes the cut glass stood out green with a slither to it as if a wire had been pulled through a green gelatin, as if the whole pane were made from the boiled bones of some underwater creature and the stuff of the animal hadn't been strained properly. And there were, like little worlds, little cavitations crushed in the medium, like immensely tiny caves. Michaux often commented on such things. Probably because, like all people who wear spectacles, he had a special relationship to glass.

Michaux Revisited

AND SO, GOING DOWN THE aisles, I arrived at Michaux's office diorama, five decades after I had last seen it. I recognized nothing. The scene, I felt sure, had changed. Michaux was so dry. And small. I was thinking, you would expect that, it's normal. But it wasn't normal.

You could see the dust in his hair. Where on earth did it come from? His neck had begun to shrink, and his collar had a gap. Yet the dignity—the dignified in him—was still there, maybe even more so, now that it seemed so private.

The cat, Jones, still lay on the chair, only her ribs had gone concave like a hammock.

And there was a "Fraught"—one of the home dioramas we'll talk about next time—on the bookshelf I hadn't noticed before, and next to all the book titles (which I had once written down in my notebook so I could find them in the library) were other, newer books I must have missed. Titles that seemed naïve, almost embarrassing: *Handy Crochet Techniques. Topiary for the Rest of Us. I Felt it in My Own Soul.*

But I was drawn to a little bookcase diorama, a tiny train scene with landscape I felt sure hadn't been there before. In it, the engine was approaching a trestle bridge (you could see the blisters of the rivets) where naked boys were jumping into the swimming hole. Two were ringed in the water, looking upward. One was poised in his dive, his small member visible. The train's headlight glowed. The train's smoke was made of cotton, teased out, dyed black. But the dye had begun to speckle off.

Then the light affect began. The 1:4800 scale drew evening into the room. Michaux shrank, then grew. The shadows traveled around his teacup. The whiskey decanter bloomed, then fell into hollows. The fire turned. An emerald feeling predominated—all of a sudden—like a forest kept in the room. Something of the rain spell was returning to the office. I leaned forward, but things were changing too fast as night fell, then dawn grew orange plates over the objects as Michaux still painted his globe, still looked at me with that perfect emptiness of expression which though it could be traced to him, was somehow not his fault. To have this representation of him stuck down here seemed mad, even cruel.

Minister Goll saw things in another way. Goll's habit was to personalize all reality. I believe he was jealous of reality: that it was outside himself. That Michaux's diorama was out of reach was intolerable. And must be personalized. For Goll the diorama, no matter the subject matter, was autobiography. Goll took from the Michaux diorama a human lesson. The suspicion arises: nothing gone forever is ever gone.

It is not known how Minister Goll came to the attention of dioramas. We say "came to the attention of dioramas" because the medium seemed to call to him, to take him over, to enchant him completely. Dioramas were "a geography of the soul," according to his speechwriter, "a duplicate vision," and a replacement for what their opponents "refuse to see": the real world. At the height of his prominence, a diorama was completed every hour in the great workshops. This went on for years, at "the edge of the human story."

I stood for some time, working things out. I could feel my attendant observing me. Now, Michaux had even more to say. Yet I could no longer hear him. It was as if the thought of Goll had made me deaf to all other sounds. I had gone beyond what I'd once known and I found that the terrain had entered folds. The distances had grown. Nothing was—everything was—the same. I came to a conclusion: the diorama itself had changed. This was the only explanation.

His paints were still glossy and wet. I gave the sign to the attendant and the room was extinguished.

III: THE CITY

Remarks

IN THE *JOURNALS*, MICHAUX WRITES how one morning in his seventh decade, he became lost in the city. He describes this experience in great detail. Somewhere between Tiln Square and the Arboretum, near the hour of two, the streetscape darkened and began to warp as if riding a soap bubble. Grotesque awnings changed color and sagged, then were pulled, long, into the sky. Suddenly, he wrote, he found himself standing in the middle of the Boulevard on the circle of green that formed the center of a roundabout. A moment before, he had been contemplating the goods in a bake shop.

He turned around, and there the shop was, set like a black gem in the bracelet of the shops, far away. But he had no memory of traversing the distance between, even as, while he watched, the shops bulged roundly like bulbs burning in a photograph, into the roadway under the carriages. Yet, Michaux still stood before them; he hadn't moved at all, and the doughed items of the bakery were expanding around the sides of his face as if to suffocate him. Standing at the same time in the roundabout, he heard the traffic as if it were far away, heard the sound of the individual grains of dust falling all around, like the eternal soft roar of rain without water. Dogs ran in the sky. The houseplants sprung flowers that were steaming the upper windows.

Now the Square began to rotate, and he with it. He reached out for a railing post to steady himself as the impulse to motion swept over all the stationary things in the landscape—the distant bridge where carriages swayed and shrank, the fall shapes of the pyramidal hornbeam along the street, the mysterious lights even now cold and null, the fountain—folding everything into the heave of the road.

Michaux staggered and held on. He closed his eyes, trying to shake that feeling of being in two places at once, but the bakeshop came forward, all the shiny bowls spreading past him on either side like the eggs of a machine as he went inside, and the dry fountain's water turned high overhead like a silver foil. Then, all at once, everything began to revolve as he himself turned in the center of the turning square—"revolving, in-volving themselves into a blob that had not yet come"—then devolving into objects so distorted they were bright and dark at the same time. Michaux felt rise in him the anticipation, encompassing all that could be seen of a "final convolution" of all the soft surfaces around him: The Great Volvarium.

It was deep night when he came back to himself. He said that he was alone in his office. He had no idea how he'd gotten there. Beside him was a sack filled with buns he'd evidently bought at the bake shop. He was sitting on his cot, and the lamp was not lighted. The museum halls were silent all around. He crept in the dark, finding the spills in the jar and touching one to what remained of the faint planets in the grate and made a light and rekindled the fire. And with slow time running out into the dark halls in all directions and the fire growing, he came back to himself and to the objects in the room.

The next day, a man asked for him at his office. The man wore a worried expression, and he held a pair of gloves, Michaux's gloves, which he claimed Michaux had given to him. Michaux had fallen down, he said. And the man claimed he had rushed to his aid and Michaux forced the gloves on him, pleading with him, saying, "Take these! Please!" Michaux had no memory of this. He tried to imagine himself in such a state of mind, in public, pleading with a stranger.

He became afraid to go outside. What if such a thing happened again? So he stayed in, trying to reconcile what had happened in Tiln Square with the dailiness of life, and spent many weeks reflecting.

Later, he came to believe that all objects were "at volvariance" with one another and that they couldn't be trusted in the mass. Yet for such an event to have happened, he decided, it would have to have had a center. Not strictly a cause—for, aside from the volvarium idea, causes were beyond him; rather, "a place of happening." He found that center in himself as a kind of blame: "I'm getting old. This happened; it resides in me," an object around which an unreal motion can be borne, not from a center or a ground precisely, but from an "irremediable selfhood not to be trusted."

He retreated into himself, there in his laboratory office. The medium, he now felt, was too "external" to admit of large things. He became fascinated with models, modeling larger dioramas in miniature or inventing new ones and putting them into boxes you could carry in your arms.

It is interesting to note that the dioramas of this time, of Michaux's Dark Period, are, though reduced in scope, some of his greatest. They reach for the evanescent, the fleeting, the grim. Dioramas which he would formerly have done at life scale with a team of assistants he now made alone in his office, as models, "immensely small." At night, he was beset by disturbing visions.

This severed hand, for instance. The skin swells around a wedding ring which digs hideously in, while a rat is cleaning it to the bone. Or a miniature of horses, burned to death in their traces, and the carriage fallen over on its side. He paid special attention to the blistering of the carriage paint, which he insisted *must not be done with fire* but with a careful change in the viscosity of the varnish. He claimed to be dealing with "the ontology of the diorama" which existed in the "emptiness of materiality."

Meanwhile, the work of the laboratory went on as before. He found himself interposing other personalities between himself and the tasks to be done. This was a boon to his staff, for his young assistants, who had dreamed of their own projects but were endlessly working under Michaux, now had a certain freedom to do their own work. And although Michaux held rights of affirmation over what the assistants would do, he found himself waving exhausted benedictions this way and that way so that the dioramas—all of which (as we shall see) resembled his work—could be done.

If a new animal had been attempted at the Farmers College or a new plant developed in all its temporary growth, everyone wanted to be the first to put it in a diorama once it died. Michaux tried to be kind. He tried to encourage. But really he drifted. He was beyond things. But he had only things. It is to this shift we owe the careful ephemeralities of his insect and shrew dioramas, his dioramas depicting the insides of drawers where the silverfish are eating the notebooks, his dioramas— two feet tall—showing the detritus in the corner of a window, with all the dried houseplant leaves individually rendered out of curled paper, spending hours getting the right mix of the planned and the accidental. As time went on, he would gaze at the "naïve" mockups of his assistants with a sort of beatified, dawning newness of expression, like a child. All dioramas were in some sense equally innocent. They were simply what they were.

Lecturing

YESTERDAY, CLARA TOLD ME THAT my lecturing tone grates on her nerves. I thanked her for this insight in a genuine way, because it's always good to be on your toes, socially speaking.

But in some sense I've known the affect of this tone all along. You see, even as a boy I would explain things to the other children, whom—quite rightly—became angry. This is because—also quite rightly—they had no ideas. They were missing the connections, I felt. And had to be lectured to. Perhaps I changed some lives in some small way.

These days, I notice the tendency in myself even more. If I order something from the butcher, either to eat or dissect—it doesn't matter—I immediately adopt a lecturing tone and before I know it I am explaining to this expert of taken-apart animals the very thing in front of them. I can hear this in my voice. And the thing is, I am simply asking for something, that is all. I can't help it. They despise me. I don't blame them for the most part.

But you see, I'm not trying to display my knowledge. I am trying to make a connection. But in so doing, I take it too far. I would lecture someone about their own name before I heard what it was.

Even during the act of intimacy, when that was on offer, I tended to want to explain things.

The Street View

I CAN SCARCELY BELIEVE ANOTHER Mote season is upon us, but there we are. The street near the Toyne Library, this year's venue, is much quieter now that the teams are inside—and the barricades, of course. I wonder who will win this time. You feel that change in the air as the influence of the game begins to manifest, and you're always tempted—though none of us is an expert—to predict the source of that change: "Ah, the mote was placed in the *Horticultural Encyclopedia, 11ᵗʰ Edition.*"

This happened to me just the other day when I noticed the hydrangea at the entrance to the Arboretum were changing color. I had read somewhere that if you introduce urine into the soil, you can change them from white to blue, but I later discovered this is just nonsense. So at the time I thought, this is the Mote, the secret silent Mote, for there the flowers were: changed. Whereas a few days before, the clumps had been a pure aluminum, folding white in the crucible of the afternoon. And I thought, "The Mote has begun to influence things." And soon, the change would enfold other objects in the world, and on it would go, and we'd grow closer to knowing...

I resolve to buy a game card tomorrow and fill it out.

Mote

THROUGH THE RAILING SEPARATING OUR balconies, Tom says that once, he almost won the game of Mote. It had been just after his wife died. On a sudden intuition and after failing with the Pigeon Loft Numbers for so long, he sent a letter to the Department of Ornithology, requesting the detailed Signal Pigeon Reports for the ten-month toss. He cross-referenced the document with department pedigree charts dating back nine years and also with the cull records of sick birds and the Pigeon Flight Record Book.

He leans forward, his mouth trembling.

"The birds were turning up in repeating flocks, Wiggins. Just as a stranger can carry the characteristics of someone you have known, and so remind you of them, the pigeons carry the memory of the pattern of their flight—across years—and among pigeons who cannot in any way have traveled the same route among the same individuals of the flock. It is as if a pattern were part of the air. And the pigeons enter this pattern as into a great, grey wheel, composed of their memory as it is dispersed among themselves and over the city."

Tom put these numbers into a greater and greater analytic. He followed their shape across time—and as a result, almost guessed where the mote had been placed.

"That's how you win Mote," he says.

Jane

WHAT'S TO BE DONE. A woman named Jane has moved in next to a man I don't much care for. A snobbish fellow who keeps to himself. He has taken out a patent for a machine that introduces pilling into fabrics by brushing and rubbing in a certain way for hours on end, which has been used extensively in the Diorama of the Town. He is very pleased with himself.

In any case, like Carla, Jane had been a craftsperson at the museum. She is a weaver in both largescale carpets and homespun rugs. She also did bed quilts for the farm cottages and the apartments of the factory workers in the Town who were meant to have quilted as a hobby.

Jane is an enormous woman with a soft face. Everywhere, she droops. As a weight loss strategy she drinks switchel, which I have learned is made from vinegar. The jar gives off a homespun odor not altogether pleasant. Her son, whom she had trained as a quilter, committed suicide not long ago and has left behind bags full of scraps, totaling over fifty pounds, and Jane's daughter, who is something of a bully and who has become obsessed with the family's history and views quilting as a means to that end, insists Jane put the scraps to use. Jane now quilts out of anxiety.

"'They can't go to waste, Ma!'" she says, imitating her daughter. The quilts are mathematical, made of interlocking squares of interlocking triangles. "I'll foist them off on someone," she says, winking.

And so it is that I acquire a smaller quilt, which I keep on the back of my chair.

In the museum, she tells me, there were pressures to weave messages into the carpets—codes and sigils, visual gestures, political messages—according to what the managers were trying to say about the figures and themes in the rooms but were determined to subsume into the overall plan. Jane resisted these demands and was, she claims, passed over for promotion. She has begun to mix wine into her switchel.

Etiolation

THIS MORNING, I RECEIVED THE last box from the office. I am not in shock at my situation but aware, at times, of a lack of shock—of a great forgetting-to-be-surprised at what has happened to me, which after all happens to everyone. And so, by virtue of the numbers, nothing has happened at all, save the feeling, in now knowing, that you've gone beyond it and failed to be surprised, at all, at what is after all intolerable but no large matter in the end.

(I'm almost grateful.)

Yet as I walk around this new part of the city, unfamiliar to me, I can't stop thinking about the project I had been working on when I received the news. I had been given no time to complete it or to pass it on to one of my younger colleagues. Furthermore, my assistant, Jeffrey, has been reassigned, severing that continuity.

And so the project sits somewhere. I am fascinated by this: the silent hover of what had been meant to be done, revolving around the ideas of the doing. Eating lunch in my apartment, I suddenly startle at something about the project that I've forgotten. I almost phone the office. And somewhere, I'm almost convinced, that project is still waiting for me.

Mosquitoes

IN ONE OF THE LITTLE dioramas scores of mosquitoes float above a water surface. They are drab as they fly, hesitating, drifting like fragile, hairlike filings brushed from a machine. Michaux has attached each mosquito to a separate sheet of the thinnest glass and then, working from back to front, inserted them in the box so that they float, interfiled madly close. Multiple planes, each with its mosquito in the twilight murk.

Near the shore of the pond, under the water, the mosquitoes have just hatched. You see them riding toward the skin, their brown bodies pop through the meniscus to stand on the surface. For the first time in their lives, they ride the sticky water. The breezes touch them. The buildings rise. On their tops are square ponds.

As you might guess, the first impulse of the mosquito is to try to return, to try to go back into the water where they were born.

But they are too slight to break the meniscus. They can't go back down, and so they stand awhile on their six legs, each with its little ball joint, like the stem of some articulating lamp, and seem to be thinking about things. To be arranging a pattern. A decision is about to be made but they hesitate to take it. They've never known the air. For them, the decision creeps, like an eternity. That is the scene before us, in this two-by-two-foot enclosure. And yet something in the mosquitoes is changing. Some impulse flutters their wings. The dust under the water is a bygone eminence. They lift from the surface and take to the air.

Department Store

ON MY EVENING WALKS, THE window displays of the Nelson Department Store, the oldest mercantile in our city, wash the pavements with soft light. Some of the displays, first conceived by students of Michaux and coming and going at the Nelson ever since, stretch along the pavement in excess of ten meters. The Billiard Room, for example, with its wax players (one of them something of a dandy with a mustache, the others old men) contains three full snooker tables, crocheted leather pockets with the balls inside. One man chalking. Slide. An elegant woman in a black dress, preparing to break, bends at the waist, beetled in the glass. The dandy's vest turns out to be of human hair, woven on a tiny loom, then dyed black. In the next window teenaged boys ski on a mountain, with smiles and goggles. Girls are painted on the backdrop, one telling a secret to another through a cupped hand. People wear woolen pants, suspenders and gaiters. The snow fell last night and is fresh. The great lodge flies its banners at the top of the mountain, behind. On and on for a full block, these scenes.

I try to ignore the man who has been following me. He's been there for two days, perhaps longer, keeping his distance. He's young, round and broad, in a suit that he has eaten and drank himself to the limits of, out beyond the window light of the pubs. Never mind.

In certain conditions at night, when a lone walker passes by, some essential change enters into these displays of commerce. Some encroachment. First of all, they are given total solitude. They are given the dignity of the nighttime and the emptied street. And as if in answer to this divestiture, they assemble themselves differently, and they become dioramas. Glowing upon the street, casting outward. And then, just as you think you've got them, they revert back.

Warrens

THE RABBIT WARREN IS A fifty-fifty diorama, meaning it is above and below ground. Two and a half acres in size and four stories tall, it is meant to be seen in the round. At one time you could climb down or go up to the vista, but now, we have to roll the ladder to the different windows. And I would have to reconstruct the vista itself (that which was once "above ground") by means of slides.

Note that silver swell of night grasses in the light of the "moon." It is evening or deep night, depending. Silver lies all across the meadow and its dome, fastening to the tree's vapor; all is in frost, and the rabbits run around the meadow every which way. Their shadows are flopped to the side and bend along the snow. In the shelter of the grass, these two groom themselves.

Then down we go. Down deep into the tunnels. How lessened the scope of the cubbies and their round nests. A mother nurses six bald fingers in the cutaway nest. The blue half-bulge of the eye, with its veins, but its seam hasn't opened, is clearly visible beneath the pink. And the numbers! In all the similar nests. The whiskers have scarcely come out of the puckers, the holes in the little snouts. Taxidermy is very difficult to do at such scale.

And here a conflict. Two males go at it as if they would kill one another. The raking gesture of the hind claws and the teeth, bared and yellow, indicate at least for one of these bucks, a change of harborage is in the offing.

But when this display stood in the museum, we would leave a

window and go about our business, not thinking anything of it, until three floors up, we would come to another window and look down, and what should we see but an enchanting night, spread out in the silver world, all covered (we could see from our new vantage) in rabbit tracks. This was *the same scene*, and it had been allowed to be large, had been allowed to extend into another window. We look through the glass with its white seeds. A single owl marks with its horns the night tree. All the tracks are set into the frost, which has become quite thick on the grasses. Above us, the stars are frozen and faint.

The world as these rabbits will come to know it passes them by, by way of our knowledge of the history of what has passed—and approaches yet again. The original world, unquote. These rabbits know no difference. The owl becomes a metaphor. It too, is fast approaching, silent in its flight.

Foetida

THIS DIORAMA ONCE STOOD IN the Mountaineering Department of the Nelson Department Store. The museum once had a rather robust system of loaning—a sort of partnership with the mercantile establishment of the City—but this relationship has fallen into disrepair due to the often odd disconnect between the dioramas and what they were being used to sell.

The phenomenon even made it into the papers at the time. When the first workers arrived, they thought someone had done a prank. A false snow had fallen. This happens to dioramas. Even the new. Even those dioramas that have been previously treated. And now, they've gone white. The indoor winter.

A strange fungus had crept upon the display. So here now is the same diorama as an empty land, with the figures removed to expedite the treatment. Indeed, *Enblancas foetida* may steal upon any diorama. In the Conservation Department, the white growth clouds the open mouth of the men and women, mouths shouting full of cotton-like clots, their arms overhead with stones that have no reason to be thrown, their armpit hairs have turned white as if they have been rolled in flour and egg. The figures are made of pigskin over a beeswax mold, and real human hair is stuck on with animal glue. Their clothing is of deer hide. All these substances, the skin, the hair and so on, have gone pale. Even the gut bowstring of this female is foamy, like curds on a horse's flank, foaming over her two fingers, straining.

This diorama, which was used to sell expedition parkas (I suppose with the attendant notion of "going into the wild"), is treated by way of adding another fungus which was designed in the Farmers College to attack *Enblancas foetida*. Then the treatment fungus dies off and is brushed away. Multiple treatments are often necessary.

Whole wings of the storage basements go white this way, and as you walk you know them by the tape blocking off the different sections. People, animals, sometimes even the landscape. Michaux made a model of the original whose figurines in their colorful landscape could fit in a two-drawer file cabinet, then chose to dust the model with powdered aluminum (the kind used as an accelerant in bombs) to simulate the fungus, even though in so doing, he destroyed the detail he'd so painstakingly created.

Winter Wolves

WOLVES TEAR APART A CARCASS: an antelope, which through the gore you can identify by its hooves.

"The frost-livid world." Michaux, from whom the phrase comes to us, appreciated this exhibit for its depiction of the cold. The wolves' snouts penetrate the dark as they approach the light of a fire, of a city. We imagine that behind us soar great heaves of blocks and windows and that these habitations are responsible for the strangeness of the dark. The moon rises behind the wolves, in that chorology of the backdrop, behind naked boughs, and clouds of iron flecks drape the sky. One wolf wears a collar.

Their bloody muzzles are done with a paint brush in napthol red—just that dusting of the hairs—looking like powder, as if they have been chewing rouge.

The alpha female "stands proud" with a broad chest on this waste ground. There are broken bricks (with the imprint *Smith &*, the partner's name buried). To the left of the female, two others are playing, one with a throat in its mouth and the other on its back, pushing with its legs into the belly of its companion. Here stands an adolescent from the year before, with that disproportionate ranginess of all youths of a certain age who haven't yet grown into their bodies. An uncertainty, almost a stupidity, and a readiness for hijinks mark his expression. As ever, several other wolves howl on the two-dimensional surface of the background. One scratches itself but seems about to join in…

Such an encounter in the early dark of the museum consists of the instant and the memory in "conjoined nilpotentcy" (Michaux meant the potency in nothingness), for whom can be said to "remember" a diorama? One moves on.

Very well, the wolves tear apart a carcass. We are given death without death. Death eats death. The dead eat the dead. A mouth with a more vitally dead and hidden mouth consumes the mouth. And so on. The present moment destroys the possibility of past destruction. That is why it feels so delicious, here in Michaux's winter. It is as if the antelope— And as you know, the Council has returned wolves to the city. There are four packs at present. They are said to keep the deer population well on the hoof.

The Ravine

YOU COULD ONCE VISIT THIS magnificent exhibit before the Fire destroyed the Smith and its attendant libraries. Only five photographs survive.

The Ravine depicts three-score sheep that fell to their death, having followed one another over the edge of the cliff in a fog. Presumably, they were in a panic over some happening in their environment.

Before the Fire all of the rocks were done in papier-mâché painted to resemble granite applied over a steel armature. Next, several species of lichen, made of pressed paper, were affixed in all their color with glue. The fogs have passed, and the sky is blue-grey. We get the sense of the distant sound of waves. The north coast of the city.

But I wish to bring to your attention the flies, covering the bodies of the sheep. And the maggots. There are even bodies of dead flies hidden in the crevasses. And on the blades of grass there are flies spying out, as it were, the chance to leap into the air. This one here is rubbing its front legs. This one cleans its eyes.

The sheep were a terrible mess. Broken open. Broken up. One is shown still alive, its eye bulging. Not one is without full treatment. Note the steepness of the ravine and the way the carcasses have been draped over the rocks. This flatness, this pliancy of recent death, is a miracle, in some sense. One can see right away there would have been no way to recover the sheep. Jeffrey has scoured the archives for newspaper stories that might refer to an actual disaster of husbandry. But he was unable to find any reference.

Michaux remarked in his notebook during the design and preparation of this great exhibit that really it was the flies, the flies alone, that constituted the real subject. No fewer than four hundred thousand individual flies were built up here, in the workshop by an ingenious method of casting in glass and the stamping of the wings out of sheets of celluloid, in order to place them on the broken bodies of the sheep, to swarm them in clouds, as if the breezes, sudden in the ravine (as if just before a summer storm), had momentarily scattered them at their labors. But here again, the flies are in the service of a larger aim at verisimilitude rather than a subject unto themselves. They have been given the respect of a treatment which the scale of the ravine cancels.

Because a fly is intimacy itself. A fly requires a room.

Mother

JEFFREY, MY FORMER ASSISTANT, COMES by the apartment today to drop off slides I'd left behind. He is a severe yet romantic man continuously on the verge of despair. This afternoon, his eyes are moist behind his spectacles. He won't stop accusing me with his eyes. I hold his hand. We stand at the balcony. Summer sleet is bouncing off the black metal and disappearing.

"You could have fought them," Jeffrey says when we're indoors.

"That's true, Jeffrey," I say, "but—"

"Oldson did so. Julia did so. And others."

"That's true."

I make tea. The ritual, from the office, hour of noon, calms him a little. I show him the flat. He stands like a board, eyeing the rooms with disbelief. I have made sure to hide all evidence of my hobby. Jeffrey responds to dioramas as if they were aesthetic objects, poetic in nature. I once felt that way, too. Though he is young, his hair is beginning to grey.

"I'm done with them," he says, finishing his tea. "Done."

"No, Jeffrey, you're just caught in a moment in time."

He removes a tiny box from his coat pocket. It contains, he says, yeast taken from a breadmaking diorama. The yeast is dormant, but it will allow me, Jeffrey says, to recreate the bread that used to be baked. I don't bake bread, but I take the box and thank him. In another compartment of the box is a vial of live vinegar, containing the mother. And finally, brewer's yeast, for port, all of which he has harvested from the forest dioramas near villages. Jeffrey has reached a level of expertise, an exile far beyond my own.

Suddenly, he jerks forward, rapt. "I could move in," he says and begins to cry.

"No mind, no mind," I say, holding his hand and then letting go. "Reality bears down, Jeffrey. You're in two places at once."

"I won't let them," he says fiercely.

"It's the newness, Jeffrey. We'll get by."

The words sound a bit hollow, but Jeffrey nods privately to himself. I don't tell him what I am thinking. What happened between us happened in the diorama.

Surgery: The Difficulty of the Fly

ALTHOUGH MICHAUX OFTEN FIXATED ON insects, some dioramas are probably ill-advised, and he should have discouraged his assistants from going forward. In this one, for example, two veterinary entomologists—from the time of the scarcity of insects—perform surgery on a fly. They are replacing the left wing, which was torn in some accident, with a wing of celluloid. The operation itself is under magnification. The veterinarians wear binocular headgear, and the diorama projects for us onto a screen (as a medical school operating theater would for a crowd of students) the procedure as seen through the scope of the doctor here. Magnified, the break on the little wing—made monstrous like a great dendronic leaf—is but a shard when seen with the naked eye. And the instruments are finer than hairs. They "neck down" as if to be but one thin pipe inside a follicle, and toward the hands of the doctors, they "neck up," till they can be manipulated by a stick that directs them this way and that, far down, where the fly is.

There is a drill with tiny bits that can be changed. A reciprocating saw operated by foot pressure, the power of which, too, is bled off, necked down, spun off on a series of flywheels operating as sinks, till the exact power needed is conveyed to the cutter.

What's to be done. This fly lived for two weeks after the operation. According to the *Journal*, the fly crawled to every corner, often resting for hours upside down at the top of the case before finally falling to the bottom. Other flies, released into the case for companionship, avoided this fly for the most part. In rare moments, it would fly in circles and then dart into the glass and finally rest on the floor of the box. It would groom the corner of its mouth as the snow fell outside, then begin to walk again.

Chrome

THE WELLFORD COLLECTION OF BUTTERFLIES, also at the Gowerty.
Genus *Therna*. The cases display the mad array of every member, male
and female, pupae, chrysalis, et cetera, of the genus *Therna*, wing to
wing. Those that disappeared from the city prior to the completion of
the exhibit are rendered in glass. Glass wings, fine horsehair antennae
painted red, gold, green as the case may be. The oldest known species
begin at the left side and work their way to the right, across the strange
shape-changes of time, as if we could read the weaver's story from the
earliest iterations in time to approach, at right, the future, the not-yet-
existing, of the genus, making their way out of the display case boundary,
out above the squares, the streets, and forming a new museum in the
mind after they have never existed and then gone extinct.

Pigeons

AMONG THE ALCOVES OF AN old skyscraper as if we were high above the cityscape, ornamental chains, carved in stone, coil in piles filled with feathers and dust. Fauna in stone peer out, curious sprites and little boys with wings in their backs, surmounted and gathered by the dark arms of the vines. The stone is done in plaster, cast from one of the buildings in the Financial District that no longer stands. The city, in one of the rare photographic backdrops, steams and smokes off into the general haze where there are ships and factories puffing into the sky in a landscape half destroyed. Michaux contributed to the little models of the buildings far below; the windows wink as you walk past.

Every ledge, every crook of vine, contains its three or four taxidermy pigeons, whom, in order to shelter from the aerial attacks of the falcon, will avail themselves of every dark place. This is quietus. The birds seem interlarded: blue jars containing themselves, waiting to be taken down.

Nearly all the pigeons have numbered bands around their ankles. Slide, please, Jeffrey. Note the stamped numbers in blue aluminum chipped and worn. The longer one looks, the more pigeons are unworked from the gloom. There seem at first hundreds in this little space. In fact, there are over a thousand in this small area. Their mauve eyelids.

On third glance, they are shabby. The mites have got at them. Even in Michaux's day, there was a call for preservation, a certain touching-up, which conservators often ignored in such cases. For they are collective, these birds. A glance will do.

We wish to go in with them. Slide the pane up and step onto the alcove ledge, our dress billowing, our tie leaping in terror over our shoulder. The window weights thump inside the wall. We leave behind all that has been necessary until now.

Bone Flock

THE DIORAMA OF THE FLOCK, unlike that of the pigeons, centers on the discovery, excavation, and assembly of the deceased birds. Now then. The clot of hollow sticks. Shards of white no larger than buttons, as if a shell road were found to have lain below our own. Billions of calcium jacks, of the sort with which children play, are the spine bones of the birds. The cause of their demise is not known. They likely dropped out of the sky all at once. The exhibit covers in some detail the possible causes.

The assembly takes over five decades.

Each bird stands or flies a skeleton over the false prairie. Smithe, in a fit of inaccuracy, said the birds must have chosen to die. They were a flock. A flock is a single thought even if it doesn't know its purpose for choosing. You can hear the hollow thrum in the room of the air circulation system, powered by bicycle from the equipment room, its flagellations of ribbon as if to allure one beyond the grate to a secret festival.

Bones. There are over six thousand birds. To reassemble the delicate orbital bones was the labor of years. They were birds who flew at night, similar to our own *Urculus* species.

Entangled

IT IS NIGHTTIME IN THE apartment. The man waits outside. I doctor my cranberry juice. I turn the lamp off, then back on, while standing in view. I feel I owe him that.

In my diorama the theen finches are poised amid some change in their coloration. I go to them. Then I lie back down. When I turn my head, the female is still yellow, but the brown cap has taken on a green hue. The male I can't quite make out. I only know he's changed.

Every leaf holds its gloss. Rain falls in the clean, black air. There is some newness there. The cries of the children swinging are stored in the rings of the park trees and come out as crickets.

Smithe, in his studies of finches, at first claimed that the birds were poised between seasons, but then, sometime during his investigations, he claimed they were not poised between seasons at all, but that they occupied two, or even three, at the same time. So that the male and the female on his feeder, which had just been replaced by two males, are actually the same, single bird at the same time in two states—in terms of seasonal plumage—and when Smithe captured one of them to verify this, all the birds died. He collected them under his feeder and discovered the exact same seeds in the exact same quantity in their crops—as well as the same genetic sequence in their cells, though, he claimed, they were not clones.

Smithe hypothesized that the finches would go about their day separately, doing separate things in different layers of time, then arriving at a specific time of day to the same basepoint coordinates, where they would peck the same seed and drink the same quantity of water, lensed over one another's intention. He repeated this experiment many times, and while many birds died, as many as were entangled, Smithe discovered something key about birds.

"This is why you often see a deceased bird in the city, there for no apparent reason," he wrote.

When I awake the next morning, the finches are still there, but they have become blue, as sometimes happens in this part of the city. I remind myself not to worry, because sometimes they flip back, or are blue and yellow at the same time.

Though I prefer yellow.

The Great Restoration

EVEN AFTER THE INITIAL EFFORTS of the Farmers College, three hundred years ago, to restore what had gone from the world, the restoration of species continues in leaps and returns. What strange animals we sometimes produce. They look backward into themselves. They sit like lumps. They can't walk. They have to be put down. But there are many successes too. For example, the grayling spawn. The migratory pigeon. And the wolves, to name just a few.

The domestic products were ready to hand: dogs, cats, ferrets, kept by people against the nighttime of empty houses. Their genetic material provided the substrate for the new wildlife of the city. It is due to these renewals that we dare not venture out unprotected at dusk. The recombination of these little ones, these pets, with the animals of the diorama produce the dream wilderness of the city. Insects. Plants, too, have been renewed, and their stems make green lenses in the dark.

It is far from extinction to atavism. From the little organisms in the murk of the canals to the great grayling spawns of our city, who, in their millions and millions, their fins so like the wings of birds swept back, have swum past nostalgia into nuisance, almost. In fact there is so much fecundity as to bile back the whole admixture of hope and geneticism. We find ourselves in a curious reversal. Slide, please.

The diorama is the very world in which these scenes were possible. And at the edges of scarcity these beasts are an enigmatic mystery. Now, we wish to yearn again, to have it back, to be able once again to love what is going away from us, to love so fiercely as to make them again.

To return to the beginning. To receive what we have eaten, wearing that with which we have clothed ourselves. The blood is drawn from one time into the decadence of another.

Only the present moment knows what's best for the future poised to reject it. Only the present moment knows what the present moment of the past mistook for beauty.

Phone Call

THE PHONE RINGS AGAIN. I have fallen asleep in my room while dissecting a kaleidoscope eyepiece. The phone rings out of that deepening surface, but when I stagger up, there is only soft noise. The line howls faintly. Insects click. I feel someone there, a consciousness, observing the sounds I make.

I recognize the personality of that telephone line. I had packed that last box a month ago, and I have no doubt someone else now occupies my office.

I hang up.

I return to my dissection. My aim is to examine the fragments of the shafts—the feather shafts trapped inside, which are semitransparent—to determine which species of bird has been used. They may accept a paper of this kind, I'm not sure.

In moments the call comes again, and this time, when I lift the receiver, I say nothing. I feel sure this is the same caller at the other end of that same, superannuated phone system I'd used my whole working life. You can't mistake that breeze; the breeze near your room, which always sounds the same, even if the room has gone away.

An idea comes to me: it's him on the other end of the line. Michaux. They are telling me, is all. They are telling me they are aware. I have caught their attention, without intending to. And so he has called. The line goes dead.

It occurs to me that my museum pass is soon to expire.

Coining

BEFORE MICHAUX TOOK TO HIS office, he had been a great coiner. "Penny on headless dove." "Blue-throated sparrow (mechanical)." The birds were a psychopomp to me, too. They really did carry the awareness of the twin world.

There was a time when I coined too. I wanted to be part of such an ennobling—I suppose you'd say—superstition. I wished to feel as if I held the light at the corners of the bricks, where the building dissolves in powdery light but as yet the sun hasn't emerged. I wanted to stand at some edge of places where our world meets the elsewhere.

Yes, I might have, when no one was looking, coined a bird.

But when is no one looking?

Be that as it may, a little oilblack dash of a bird, having struck a window to the left of the fire escape, was my first. After that, an elligneous sparrow, our most common bird, plain red with a brown crest. Each got a penny. I liked fresh pennies, as if there were no secrets there.

The Whale II

THE WHALE DIORAMA RISES IN the empty museum. I have returned in the early morning to beat the crowds. Toward the bottom of the resin is a teacup, its bottom like a bell, turned toward the viewer. The saucer floats deeper in the murk, and the whales are so large, you almost miss that "white barnacle broken off the idea of the ship." The teacup as if detatched from a giant squid, drifting.

Close enough to the glass to read, the cup bottom bears the usual potter's marks, along with, in blue glaze, the code $SN3348d^{(0)N2}$. I write it down, displeased with myself for having missed it before. Against my hunch, I search for others in the spilled items of the ship's domestic quarters...but only that saucer, too far away to read, holds what might be another number. And when I check the description in the catalogue record, hoping to find an inventory of the objects and the materials used, I find only a reference to "cup and saucer." Though I try, I find no original alphanumeric in the resin, no subsequent code to tie this restoration to other dioramas. Had Michaux meant for it to be the beginning?

But that number. $SN3348d^{(0)N2}$. He'd hidden the code *as part of the diorama*. The d for "down." The zero in parentheses, and the mysterious appendage, N2, "North 2." Intended for the pattern, to be sure, though whether this is just a bare continuation of the sea or a part of some other plan, I don't know. The number had gone inside. This was the secret Goll had taken into his own project. The personal geography.

My heart sinks. Why had the phone call come? Why had I imagined that instruction, to come here, if indeed I had? Why do this to a person?

On the mezzanine, as the first of the schoolchildren arrive like little dots far below, I take in that enormous cube, looking for the seam of the original cube—on which there had been no number—taken from the rubble. In the morning light, it appears as a semi-transparent foil, on a shivering diagonal the whales occupy. And the silvery, rough parts are visible only from a distance, as a sky gone to live underwater. I go home.

IV: AFTER MICHAUX

Interlude: Theater Odeon

A CHANGE FLOWS OVER THE theater: a deep quiet descends. The air has gone heavy, it is midway through the evening. "Some change in the air." Something has occurred out there, among the seats. The darkness crowds round. This strikes him as odd, since it is he, Wiggins, on the stage. Yet he's sure the light hasn't changed. Meanwhile, a great length of time is running outward toward the last sound.

And in the silence a second awareness slips.

The audience has vanished, and there is a figure watching him. A single figure. Just above. First tier. Wiggins can feel this figure, in a coat and a high collar, fixing him in place.

Wiggins's mouth has gone dry and he can't speak. He knows only that he must continue. That figure—that man—mustn't know, mustn't know Wiggins knows. His finger, miles away, has locked on a few jagged notes by way of an outline on the lectern.

The people have gone up into the general heat, become vapor and risen through the transoms into the night rain. And now, an entire room gathers around their absence, and the question becomes, what now. It seems to him, while the figure of the man leans, that some newness has been taken from its envelope to be displayed this evening.

A plangent green comes gradually down at the edges of his vision, spilling, and the forest of the city outside the doors, that space of the Horticultural Mandate, drips without sound; only, without the damp drops behind the collar and the catkins swirling in drains. A dry rain, falling indoors. Artillery thumps in the distance. Ah. They must be shelling again. The grayling are spawning soon, into the pools. That swarm of bodies, that high fin like an airfoil. Surely Jeffrey hasn't gone? He searches for the booth high up but can't see it through the membrane of the light.

He mustn't open his mouth. Don't embarrass yourself, not now of all times. Keep it together. Get through it. It's a question of habit.

He reaches his hand, someone else's hand, out for the glass of cranberry juice. He brings it to his lips, a jewel become huge, and red, and drinks. The acidic scald of the mixture is familiar to him. The figure knows what's in it, has been following all these weeks on account of it. There's a mild sneer up there. The people he's known, perhaps. Their disapproval. There's a fleshiness spreading over the teeth. The fleshiness. He takes another sip. This alone anchors him. The green curtains are lifting. He sets the glass down on the lectern edge. What's to be done. He clears his throat.

"Now then."

At the sound of his voice the man disappears, the audience returns, and in the space of a breath the hundred mustaches whistle their little peeps, and the feathers of hats and programs churn in the waterfalls of the air. It is as if a wing has risen between beats and an avian scapular gives the impossible structure, and the warmth of the bird under the pert, cold feathers, shaped as a bubble headlong for flight, arches overhead as plushes and human watchers, clothed in shirtfronts and dresses, all fluttering equally in the "world breath," marking their passage, thrum. A wave travels over him of dry light, pollen, motes. He's certain he'll collapse right there. Down he'll go onto the stage, under the screen with a diorama on it. He'll hit his head. Gripping with his hands, he rides out the dizziness. He leans forward, searching for that earlier figure, but indeed, it seems to have gone away, although Wiggins senses a wry smile from somewhere off the edge of the night. He blinks. He swallows. He reaches for the presence of those friends, down front, whose faces blend into the lemon wall.

He smiles, somewhat. Snow seems to blow for a moment, then passes.

"Bit of a spell—"

A familiar voice calls for water. Is it Jeffrey?

Wiggins peers into the booth, where that lean silhouette and its Adam's apple, its collar and tie are still and frozen. Jeffrey remains at his post.

"No, no," Wiggins replies, tapping the cranberry. "This little fellow is quite adequate, thank you.

"Now then…"

Toward the Present Day

IT IS TEMPTING TO SAY that after the death of Michaux the nature of reality changed. But the diorama has always been our chief mode of depicting the world—since that first discovery of the whales, glowing like a glacier under what would become our city. More than literature, more than law, the diorama has been the philosophy all along. Jeffrey, feel free to do the slides freeform. Like butterflies, as the man said. I don't see there's any other way.

Recently, I visited the Ptern Annex where the new dioramas, as part of a retrospective treatment of the medium, are under construction. The rooms were of all sizes, from cubbies to fields of view; the workers coming and going in a quiet bustle. Items floated by on trundling carts and in the hands of assistants. Clumps of grass through the hallway swept back like hair. One worker, as I watched, carefully tilted a pool of blood backward onto a handtruck and wheeled it away. A woman stood high on a ladder brushing a blue color into the sky with a light touch, "As if she were trying to wipe something into—or out of— existence." I moved on, farther into the silent exhibit. Nothing had been done here. All was white. A change was about to happen, but as yet it hadn't come.

After Michaux, the permissions began to assemble, the permissions for chaos, a delightful chaos one doesn't know quite what to Do With. Michaux was a unifying figure in the medium—through him, you put "things" inside the rooms in all their personal (which is to say, Michaudian) detail. The influence of his quiet personality gave us the forest world beginning to grow there: autobiography as love, without consequences.

Retherford said our attraction to Michaux is a nostalgia for Being and a nostalgia for the diorama of the mind. We have grown since Michaux. We have changed. As to how we got here—well—one doesn't know how the world edges toward the grand and total organization of Goll. We can't quite grasp it. But we can examine the debris.

Conceptual Dioramas

CRITICS POST MICHAUX COMPLAIN OF a "new reticence" and fussy intellectualism. They accuse later practitioners (though not Goll) of a morbid fascination with the Hidden.

Post-Michaux dioramists are credited with inventing the following Conceptual Dioramas. This is of course not an exhaustive list: Dioramas that Change (by mechanical means and tricks of light (in contrast to mere animatronic dioramas) (animals will be put in and taken out from one day to the next), Empty Dioramas (depicting things that have been pulled from the display but still exert a presence), Dioramas of Absence (which create a diorama in the mind without there being a referent diorama), Dioramas of Scale (always) (the displays being of every conceivable size, down to the microscopic), Relational Dioramas (which aim to show the interconnectedness of things), Object Dioramas (where an object stands in for an entire history and creates a story), Dioramas of Evocation (meant to inspire political, mass emotion), Utilitarian Dioramas (which are used in the courts of law to this day), Fraughts (for home display), Insurance Dioramas (to record the possessions of a home, not to be confused with the Sanborn Insurance Dioramas of city buildings), Puzzle Dioramas (directed at children), Dioramas of Process (usually three or more in a linked series), Surgical Dioramas (to be implanted in the body), Novelty Dioramas (popular among our great-great grandparents), Nested Dioramas, and of course the Zoetropic Advertisement Dioramas that create the illusion of motion as the subway train, gaining speed out of the dark station, passes the niches in the tunnel.

I saw one just the other day on a journey to an unfamiliar district, where an ideal male figure, his torso indexed perfectly, was moving from one side of an opulent apartment to the other. He was gesturing in an elegant morning robe. His hands made occult gestures, he was signaling with his draping hands, but due to a mistake in the speed of the train, I couldn't figure out his intention. I would come to know that man over the weeks. I would see him again and again in the tunnels.

The idea, as Michaux once wrote, was to "see what could be done."

Zoetrope Man

THE M LINE EXPRESS HURTLES through the underground station. Figures in attitudes of surprise, stepping back, looking at their watches, white columns, then the deep tunnel again. And to my surprise the man—in the zeotropic advertisement—appears outside the black window, awash in yellow light, moving through the room in his robe. I have rediscovered him. He is moving across the room on the other side of the glass. He is moving his lips to me. He is speaking. Looking right at me. Before I can react, he vanishes down the tunnel. Indeed, his appearance is so brief, so instant and full of light, that I have to convince myself he was really there.

This is not my regular subway line. I am heading to complete my paperwork at city hall, to pay a fine incurred when I had forgotten to prune the serviceberries on the west side of the building and for which I'm responsible. Then, come to find out, I had pruned them incorrectly, causing another level of fines. And then I had forgotten to sign the form which brought on another violation and I keep having to go back and forth, over the weeks. And each time, beyond Station Lepp, the underground man winks into existence in the window, selling his wares. I have to piece him together from the trip before. The advertisement is made up of seventy-two separate dioramas, and the train, moving at a speed of twenty-four alcoves per second, gives movement to the man within. I am disturbed that his lips move. I had not noticed this the first time, and I doubt it now. In between trips, I've got to wait, carrying this possibility in my head.

Historical Dioramas

YET ALL DIORAMAS ARE FOUND. Mary Retherford came to this belief one day at the Ptern when she happened upon the exhibit of a melted bell that had fallen through its tower during the Fire. Now nothing more than a tortured shape, carbon adhering to the bronze (or is it brass, I can never figure), the bell resembles a blob anemone crawling on a beach in a green struggle. She could feel a presence all around her. And that presence was the Fire. Recall, the fire burned so hot that buildings burst into flame a mile away. Huge boards flew in the air, on fire, before the fire even got there. Thus, the cold bell is a display of fire, burning as a scene.

Objects have awareness, and they are haunted. Not "they haunt"— Retherford was clear about this. They are haunted. I search for the bell in the museum's storage catalogue. My fingers pull at the cards in the drawer, and they make fitful, snapping sounds because they are so tightly packed. I continue for some time looking for that signal card: BELLS (MUNICIPAL)—FIRE—SOCIAL ASPECTS, to no avail.

The Gun

RETHERFORD'S MOST FAMOUS DISPLAY IS probably the cross-section of a muzzle loader recovered from the Battle of the Fifth Ward centuries ago. Cut in half longitudinally so we can see what's inside the barrel, the weapon is shown full of wad and ball and powder, wad and ball and powder, nearly full to the breach. The explanatory matter gives the tale.

The Battle of the Fifth Ward was so violent and so loud that when the soldier fired and the weapon failed to discharge, she had no idea. She couldn't hear. She pulled the trigger. There was no kick, but she didn't know. She crouched and reloaded. The weather reports indicate heavy dew, which caused the caps to fail. And likely, there was the problem of haste. So the soldier fired again. And again the weapon failed to discharge. And she didn't know. Firing again and again until the barrel choked with balls and wadding and powder, all packed one on top of another.

Heat. Sound. Calm gone wrong. The muzzle loader is an exhibit of absent sound.

Once found, such exhibits make themselves. You need a mere cataclysm. Exhibits such as these have the added merit of being what they are. Admittedly, the cross-sectioning of the muzzle loader creates a twin weapon which can be displayed elsewhere, exactly as its twin, if you like, by the other side. But we needn't think of that when we're imagining the battle. Retherford kept a photograph of the weapon tacked above her desk.

The explanatory matter for the muzzle loader informs us that the weapon belonged to a girl of fourteen. She has carved her name on the stock, and we can track it back to the rare—very rare—army records of the time. The fighting had gone on, street to street, for weeks. The girl was posted at the improvised picket in the Fifth Ward (across from the old Nelson Department Store), firing across the legs of chairs and carriage frames, into the Arboretum. We imagine young Sara Witherspoon firing that weapon in an act of courage or automatism and not knowing, unable to tell because of the great sound, she wasn't firing at all. We're pleased she kept firing anyway; it seems an act of heroism. There is blood on the stock. We know it isn't Sara Witherspoon's because the type, B positive, doesn't match the girl's, which according to the army records was O negative. So now we have blood all round her, and smoke. The thing forms. The hidden thing.

I'd have thought Retherford would have rebelled against such intimations of "story." To have the object alone and naked and sending out waves was more her way. Yet she knew. She knew. The most important things about the diorama are no longer visible.

Zoetrope Evening

I WAS CORRECT. THE YOUNG man's lips are moving again. In those seconds in the roaring train, I try to figure out what he's saying. In a flash, he's gone. Since I last saw him, they've stapled him into evening wear, holding a drink, one pinkie raised, the white shirt and the cufflinks setting off his golden hair and his teeth, sparkling-flashing at what certainly must be the limit of all dentition. There is a seam around his mouth, all the way around, as if he has forgotten to shave, like the movable lips of a puppet.

Another day, he is no longer alone. They've given him a cat—call her Charles, you might as well—an elegant longhair with a contemptuous gaze riding his arm with perfect aplomb, limbs draping down. With green-eyed flatness it yawns, slowly, the mouth opening. The yawn shuts at the last diorama, and the plunging wall goes black into the side-sweeping tar passage: pointing by way of the trainwindow-splash, the sooty safety-alcoves blipping by.

The cat's yawn is perfect, as he administers the pink flower of its boredom to the benumbed passengers of the train, reading newspapers, serial paperbacks, a sandwich paper-torn, open on a knee, smelling of yeast and pickles, all conjoined by yawn-logic's implacable hard pallet of ridges, teeth and pinknesses, all ashine, and fresh.

Before he cut off, the young man was drifting his drink-hand in front of his body. His lips kept moving. He is one of those men who speak while smiling, to pull you in, while offering you the indifference of his cat. The train clashes its silverware, all around. He speaks, I feel, only to me. Over the weeks I pay attention, sitting on the edge of my seat in anticipation of his arrival. I set it up so I'm the only one there. And all at once, he floats, he approaches the window, too close. I lean away, fearing he will cross over and I will smell him. His eyes twinkle. He has something, a secret. The speed of the train is right this time. I feel he will convey his message.

Relational Taxidermy

WITH RESPECT TO THEIR INVOLVEMENT in the Colne District Project of Relational Taxidermy, practitioners sought to examine the fixed nature of a locality. They asked, "What passes through?" And in your passage through a given place, how can you know what was once there? What traces remain, and to what scale are you prepared to go to find out? Mary Retherford called investigations of this kind, "backtracking." The way it was done was to examine in great detail a small area—one hundred meters square—in order to discover the plants and animals that had died there. This was Relational Taxidermy, named after the tendency of things to be interconnected.

As we have seen, every object wears a skin. Fair enough. This skin removes itself over time and is dispersed. Each object remains as a net with its molecules growing farther and farther apart, changing oftentimes into other proteins, but always a net. As one net spreads, she said, becoming thinner and thinner, another net coalesces to a fixed point and begins to spread in kind. As many as you like. Jeffrey? Slide?

Now then: the Retherford Laboratory. An unnamed dioramist stands at the lab table in a white coat. To her right, a simple preparation stretched over a mold but not yet glued down. A rather useless cat (our apologies to poor Charles). The glass eyes are missing and the eyeholes merely slits. But note, just off to the side in the background. In this enlargement we can just make out the edge of a shape, pressed against the baseboard molding. The strange mass no photograph could capture. Here, the mass appears close-up, grotesque. A dried paste, clotted with hairs. Little bones. Crystals gleam, impossibly tiny, as if it were a giant pellet from the throat of a great horned owl. The threads of some fabric fray off into nothingness. This great pile of detritus, no larger than a horse lying on its side, was collected from the Colne District and analyzed, bit by bit, under microscope, flake by flake. Flecks of skin: of bats, it turns out. A black powder from some ancient fire, prior to our own Great Fire. Some tweed traced back to a design eighty years old, dropped somehow down the black shaft of a pantleg. Crumbles of red brick indicating a building of which no other trace remains.

The Colne had been bombed many times. Among the shell fragments, they found a churn of the layers which otherwise would have been intact and placid. So they had to be sorted.

Into that zone of one hundred square meters Retherford and her assistants poked and tweezed. They found evidence of insects recently extinct. The milk teeth of raccoons came out of the soil. Dander of men and women preserved in a small place out of the damp. Hairs. Cinderized wood that was believed to have been an ancient wind-brake when this was a field.

All quite predictable. You sort of know what you'll find (which is the chief problem of such inquiry). "How long will we be at this," her assistants, many of whom quit, wanted to know. "Until we're done."

How, they asked, do we make a *real preparation* (meaning a taxidermy) of an animal that has been killed, dressed, cooked and eaten? How far back is it possible to go, given the evidence, and how small down? Is there a way to track back to what things were, beyond even the field's obscurity and to know? At what point can we still build the animal from what's left? Isn't there, they said, always some piece of life, however small, left behind? In all the fires that have ever been in the city isn't there still some particle of every fire blowing high and cold in the atmosphere? Everyone who has ever been burned alive or taken out and shot against a wall, isn't there some evidence, high up and however far away, of their last statement for and against themselves?

Zoetrope Speaks

WELL. HE BECOMES SOMETHING OF an event in my day. I watch his lips in the three-second light, and I grow—the more I see him—more unaccustomed to him. Each time, he is more distant. Each time he speaks to me, he says less, and yet more. I find this most immediate, most consensual.

I am curious to know him. I want to know a person who receives so much attention with such nonchalance. His chest so broad, his hair a blond of total absurdity. I was not sure at first, but I have decided he is changing over time. Every few days he bends a little more at the waist. His skin is darkening. Each time. Then they lighten it again. His shirt a little dirtier, gone gray with the particulate black of all subway tracks and tunnels, that oily substance from the secret fire. And here he is turning his wrist over, while he looks at me, and pointing to something. I verify this the next day. He is pointing to something I missed. Wearing that smile, the lips closed now on the word he has been uttering, his eyes half-closed in contentment at what he knows. See there, he says, over there, in the corner of the room? Then—all at once—he's gone again, into the howling tunnel. I imagine him pressing against the glass with his cheek and his palms, like a comedian pretending to be frantic, to complete what he has to say to the black and frosty stars, cold stars streaming behind the shaking yellow streaks of the reflections, at the shaking horizon line. Those stars have no name I know. I will have to see him again. To confirm all of this. There really isn't any other way, Jeffrey.

Squirrels

IN OBJECT DIORAMAS, ANIMALS BEGAN to be used as objects unto themselves; their "environment" was gradually moved into the space between.

For example, in this one, eleven taxidermy squirrels in a progression occupy the space between one tree limb and another, jumping the gap of about twelve feet, to show the different positions through which a squirrel goes when it jumps. For one squirrel to jump, twelve go into the diorama as proof of motion. The final squirrel is miraculously the same size as the first. He has just struck the bough, and bent it down, bent the stem deep downward, tail bushed out and cocked wildly sideways as the creature gains balance. The stomach is butter-colored and the rest reddish brown. Slide, please.

But there is one more squirrel, off to the left, resting on its haunches with the typical acorn gripped between its hands and the whiskers flared to the sides: the tail is now laid on the back in an S curve, and he fixes us with a disinterested, but alert, eye. This final squirrel has almost nothing to do with the previous twelve. Immaculately separate, each of the thirteen from all the others, each is identical, and we can't find a single flaw. Each must be identical, even down to the scar on the left, rear paw, which presumably one of the specimens had and so all must have.

The card beneath it indicates that this diorama is one of the first to imitate the photograph, in this case "motion capture." We are not surprised when we learn photographs were the point of origin: a single squirrel caught, again and again, in a single jump. Here is the source picture. The little fellow was somewhat obese, which suggests he was tame. The black background in the diorama, too, is the same. There is no alternative way to do this diorama. The result of an accurate portrayal would be a monstrous, elongated fur, with eyes and a tail, in the shape of the arc. The blur of life. And in the end, you wouldn't save on squirrels, because to cover the gap you may well need eighteen, twenty of them, sewn together.

Thus, there is a deep comfort here. The notion that "The squirrel's leap is committed to the pattern but different every time in the great pageant of life." Our squirrel jumps once for all eternity. That's something we can hold to.

Etymologies

HAD IT NOT BEEN FOR his lips and what they were doing, I would've had no need to return to the man in the tunnel. You see, you only realize what has gone on after the event is over, all the events in their sequences.

I discover his intention while I am in my apartment. All those times, the young man, he was speaking a word or a set of words. Why I had ignored this, I don't know. But now, the lips close on a consonant, then open ever so slightly, the tongue touched downward. Then the teeth come softly together and the lips retract from the teeth in a soft, unconscious sneer he hasn't intended. I know right away that first shape must be a P or a B. But the vowel—I'm certain there's only one—eludes me. Without doubt, though, the last mouth shape, when the teeth come together and retract the lips almost to what I now think is a smile, is an S. Over the trips, which I'm embarrassed to admit I keep going backward by train to suss out, I determine that middle sound can only be an A. That seam around his mouth, the flesh is a slightly different color, like you find with dirty flesh-rubber, a hollow behind, to accept the new mouth, which they use to change his expression. They take the different vowel shapes out of a suitcase with compartments of velour, the mouth stranded one lip from another, the tongue floating in the dark, the plosives and whatnot, and the mouths, complete with teeth, rest inside the case, swinging at the end of a handle near someone's thigh as they walk through inky positionalities of many stations. This one, I think—the teeth cover the lower lip, fricatively and zip out of sight—is almost decipherable. He wants to speak. And as he communicates, the signal is broken into so many different pieces, it feels—but I will come to it, I will meet them as they come together as they certainly must—I will meet him halfway.

Novelty Goods

Now THEN. A BIT OF a shift: toward commerce. Dioramists after Michaux found many ways to commercialize the small—and especially the tiny—displays. Even today, you can sometimes find such items in antiques shops.

Human figures can be seen inside the surface of these shirt buttons. They bend over hearths preparing food. Crystalline flames touch the little black pot as the woman stirs. Hand in hand in traditional outfits and worn-out shoes, they greet the sun coming over this tiny hill.

This man shoots ducks, in different stages of the business. Reminiscent of Dioramas of Process, these buttons progress down the shirt front, showing the duck hunt. In the first button, the man with his earflaps and the retriever crouching in the blind, the decoys— absolutely microscopic—perch on the lake. In the next button, ducks in the silver morning air, skimming high. Then the shot—and the duck struck, draping in the sky. The duck limp on the water in the center of wave rings. Sending the water dog. He's in mid-leap, front paws tucked. The duck held at last, draping in the retriever's mouth. Of course, you can't quite see what they are, they were so small—best enjoyed with a hand lens.

But, you see, people at the time knew they were there, in the buttons. More than one diarist at the time describes the feeling of a close crowd, of being pressed close to a person, and the buttons huge as the sky, floating past, a strange odor rising, the odor of human skin.

Or here is the scene of a marriage in the side of a cigarette lighter and meant as a talisman. It shows a man knifing a woman, his arm back for the strike. The caption reads "REVENGE" in block letters.

Barrettes and the little balls connected to hair ties were also a popular scenic place. As ever, the scale was the chief joy. The wonder of a thing so small. Friends jump rope together. They play patty cake. These two little girls climb a wall at the top of which is a cat, watching them. In another hair tie, this one for a woman, the white chickens, surrounded by air bubbles, peck around the farmer's wife in her apron, who disperses the cracked corn, the chopping block off to the side with its tiny stuck feathers and the two nails driven in.

Dioramists also experimented with humorous scenes at the bottom of beer mugs: subaqueous games (buxom barmaids and all of that) on the theme of ebriety, but these were controversial because they privileged right-handed people, (for left handed people the figures were all facing away), and until the innovation of total encasement in glass, were difficult to clean, besides. But they would glow when hung up on their rods in the tavern, the laughing shrieking mouths of the subjects cut to worms by the glass.

Later, companies came out with candy scenes. Candy balls that you would patiently suck to reveal a clear candy globe scene in the middle, in which was housed a puzzle diorama. Chocolate shells with forest scenes, or farms, or this building-top home, complete with microscopic furniture cast in boiled sweets. In other cases the candies were put into dough, then fried, sprinkled with sugar and sold on the street. You were supposed to eat carefully and discover the figurine in its room, inside. They were done in some detail, sometimes excruciatingly precise, which was spoiled by the encasement in the dough and by the transparent nature of the candy. And by the tendency of the sweets to distort if you overfried them. They could deform gruesomely, as the hands of this man—and his face—clearly show.

Not to mention the fact that you *ate* these people.

As a giant would, striding over the districts, smiling and waving.

Fraughts

DIORAMISTS, OUT OF DESPERATION AT budget cuts, returned to fraughts after having abandoned them. Designed for home or office, they take up a small space on a shelf and are excellent bookends. Turning to the materials on hand, the dioramists began to saw up the animals and to assemble them as "excerpts" of reasonable size and sell them into home libraries. This example, designed for a deep bookshelf, lends a sylvan feel to the leather volumes.

In the little case a deer leg is severed at the tibia, stepping over the mosses at dawn. We are positioned down low as if we were a toad watching the great stem of the leg go past. Strange plants overfeather the view—bracken fern and jack-in-the-pulpit (only slightly changed, as if they evolved in some other place). Three shy mushrooms, like polyps, seem almost shellacked; you can almost see the glass recurved on their cap-tops. The hoof of the leg with its black gloss like the top of a lab table splays as it steps on a pile of droppings. One or two pellets are crushed, revealing their lighter insides. The tendons of the leg bulge, and the veins are like distended rivers made of sand in some desert, disappearing around the back.

Speech

It is clear after several more trips: the message is a single word. It can only be—it must be—BASS. Which is absurd. All that trouble for a fish. Or, if you like, for a lower note they're tricking you on. They show the fish, but you're expected to hear the other etymology, underneath, the bass note, the thing it's resting on. I cast the idea aside for PASS. The new word is an acknowledgement of my behavior in the train—of my attention and my attempt. They're saying I'm trying. I am going and he is staying. I go by. And on my own adventure, in my passengership, I really am. I see that I am. I pass. At the same time the word holds a warning within. I am, they are saying, to leave off, to quit this venture, right away. Go by. Leave it alone. The young man now leans down to me, he is whispering what I know him to be. I am to pass by. As I pass I am to leave off. There are things to be pruned, up there, in the windbrake.

I sit with my hands in my lap. I make it home, my coat over my arm, without seeing anything at all, though I am vaguely aware of the machinery of bird calls screeching without bearings in all the wheel hubs in the hollows and the dusty clops. At home, I make tea and I put something in it as a matter of attention to detail, as a condition of practice. I am looking out the window with the blank silvergold windows and the turning wind roses of the empty balconies opposite. Then, I suppose because I've stopped trying and am well within myself, the truth comes to me, the truth of that word, in its potential slide...

There is a different one in there, in the detachable mouth of the young golden man, and that word—I fail to understand why I didn't see it before—is MASS. Somebody has gotten a fingernail into the seam and worked it loose. "The necessity of a weight." Some object interior to itself, some waiting thing out there or in here, it wouldn't matter among the available envelopes at present, is coming out of the suitcase with the mouths. "A weight." And somebody, some teacher, would tell you at this point that weight and mass are not the same thing. The latter is a far more serious matter, far more intrinsic. I hear Tom shift in the chair around the corner, behind the railing. The sun is going prettywell down. I hold my breath and listen.

**

It is the middle of the night. There's nothing for it. The thing's been done intentionally-on-purpose. The young man would be speaking all along in the howling rattle of the opposing trains. There would be no reason for him to stop. But now they've given him a new sort of permission. Someone else is doing this, someone who has been communicating to me in this way, and my mind sinks at the obviousness of the whole thing. It's all gone wrong. I can't stop thinking about earlier in the day, the last time I saw him. And in that instant, nightflying in the tunnel, the car reflections of handstraps and poles crowding the windows like medical devices, I had seen a department store worker: a man hiding his face, shoulders hunched, holding a paint roller against the wall, to pretend to work. A red handkerchief in his back pocket.

I sit up in bed, thinking the word must have been FAST. It might really have been FAST. The way the lips come together; I missed that little fricative. He is telling me I have to hurry with my investigations. My museum PASS will soon expire. Or I'll meet with an accident when nothing can be proven.

I could go back, to be sure. But first, there are other places I have to go.

V: THE LIBRARY OF CANCEROUS TUMORS

Reading Room

I TELL NO ONE I'VE come here. Least of all Jeffrey. This place is for scientists and specialists rather than for the generalist like me. But you pay a small fee and you can go in, out of the summer and into the freezing building. You feel the cold through the thighs first, through the thinness of the wool. There is the feeling of a sort of destiny when things are frozen.

Michaux once sat on the board of the Library and to his misfortune toward the end contributed many specimens to the collection, cut out of him during an illness he in fact survived, only to be killed by something far stranger, dark and planetary, that hasn't found a name anyone can agree on, even to this day.

A lone old woman sits at the far end of the table under a lamp repeated in green bells all along the center, with a chain of little brass pellets hanging down. The woman presides over a small, white snow-covered ball on a tray. Her hand goes into her bag, there is a crackle, her hands untwisting something. Into her mouth goes a candy. Then a companionable silence settles between us. I do not ask her why she is here, and·she does me the same courtesy.

They do a bag-checking procedure at the security box because once, there was a man who stole the tumors to take them home. He would cook them in sauces and eat them. He was one of those devil-may-care hermits with a rare sense of humor. When officers asked him for heaven's sake *why,* he said he was only trying to be healthy.

In prison he died of cancer.

The Wall Boy

A SINGLE WINDOW, HIGH UP in the wall, holds back the pressure of the cold storage beyond the atrium: miles and miles of shelves, the tumors frozen wet, yet alert. I imagine the room behind that high window as a kind of lunch area for staff; a single man alone at a table reads a sandwich and eats a book, his hands blue and wet. In here the pressure of that cold storage looms down over you, and your nose drips. Faint fogs hang in the air, as in a forest of light, without trees of any kind, only that inclined plane of a sunbeam, strung on lines of frost, wet and taut, ending on the floor mosaic: the seal of the Ministry of Culture.

I pause on a card describing a six-hundred-pound tumor that had grown in the side of a little boy. I remember him. He became something of a medical celebrity. The papers featured him, thin and hollow with a round head in a hospital gown and holding a plush alligator, next to the tumor that was scheduled to be taken out the next morning. The surgery was a dicey affair. That afternoon, across the baking city through the dust of midsummer, the radio gave updates between the symphonies and the news. We crowded round when the music ended and the voice barked out. There was some problem with the vessels, the way they were intertwined. The surgeons were working inside him, as at the untangling of a loom. Then, all at once, at four, the surgery was over, the boy recovering with, they said, "an expression of contentment." He was asking for the universal, transparent substance at the utmost center of all recovery: gelatin, flavored with strawberry. All went well for him in the end. He lived to be an old man and once, on his ninety-ninth birthday, posed in the paper next to his tumor, which had been trundled into the lobby for the purpose of the photograph. I recall his serious expression, concentrating skeletally, and his glasses. No hat, no tie. A head bald and spotted. His hand rests on his hip, and his hip hitched out, as he leans toward the thing big as a boulder in a pasture, exactly as if he invented it, like an engineer next to a newly designed bomb that will change the course of history, until he is sped away in the whirr of the microfiche.

Michaux's Tumors

THERE ARE MANY TUMORS, WITH booklets describing them. I sit for some time listening to a great bulb of meat before me. About the size of a loaf, pink snow foams over a surface burned with crystals. Under, muscle-like striates merge into blue and yellow blobs of flesh covered in polyps. One end glistens, broken open to a burned surface as if it has come impossible distances to get here. Biopsies mark the top—plugs taken out—and evidence of precise dissections. At the other end a clean plane has been struck away, leaving a mirrorlike surface in which you feel you can see things. The card on a string reads: 616.99 / RC254.5 TUMORS—HUMAN   (MALE)—PECTORAL—MICHAUX, H.L.—SOCIAL ASPECTS.

The tumor has no odor to speak of. If it does smell in some way, I would say I'd like it to smell unfamiliar, like something left long ago in a box, rather than something new. The air around it has been combed by an imaginary wind, passively, tumbling the locust tips out there, they sway back, the sticks, dark against dark cloud, to the way they were before. Examining all the booklets, I read about these things that Michaux has produced with such enthusiasm inside himself. Nothing, it seems, ever got near the man without becoming more than it had been before it reached him.

This was year two of his struggle. Michaux first felt it when he awoke in the middle of the night. A strange pressure in his chest, and palpitations. Like all diarists he takes a little bit of time to describe the moon, "the only thing that can be trusted," streaking as a passenger behind the clouds. He details the exact pains needling out from his ribcage, "down toward the groin." He issues himself words of encouragement, mixed with a certain stoicism. He won't leave off, he says—not now—not now that he is beginning to know things. He will try harder. He promises himself. It would be unfair not to, unfair to the "strange affirmation of life" forming within him.

Turning a page, I recall Michaux's statement about all these masses hidden on the shelves: They are not things from animals. They are *potential* animals.

They are becoming.

The Mind of the Tumor

THE FOG CLINGS TO THE wool of my coat and freezes in particles like stars. They say a vapor rises in the city. They say that this is why, that this explains the contents of the library. Deep within and long ago, they had done something extraordinary, these people, in the black cube of their mind. The observation window is encased in ice, around the edges frosted with our breath. But toward the middle hurries a black ice, the parts of the river where the water is close to the surface and great, warping bubbles hollow by on their way across. I can't see what moves under there, but there are suggestions of the huge swells of grayling all atremble, swaying in the flow.

I recall just now that the Farmers College has released a new apple. Green primarily, with black inklike swirls. Tastes like spring, they say, and cleanses the liver.

Asteroids

HERE ON ANOTHER TRAY IS a host of little frozen blue snowballs, taken out of him all in one go. This one is a tiny skull swept by blue hair. That one a feverish tulip bound up in spirals of fleshy growth.

I begin to scrape. I brush the crystals into the tray. The scraper and brush are gentle, softer than the stonelike tumors.

This one is from the lining of the stomach, which has been removed with the tumor. He ate through a tube afterward. I can see, like a piece of yellow glass, the mucus lining. That part of the stomach has become something else, completely gobbled up, replaced, welcomed into a frantic mouth.

This one rests on its side, peeled raw like a grape, revealing the vessels like red plants pressed flat under the current of a river. A piece of silk stitching is stuck to the surface.

This one resembles nothing so much as a can of soup that has been slithered out of its tin while cold, only to collapse down without losing its shape, the ridges of the can (perhaps the imprint of his ribs) fitted into its body, while this littler one is a tidy red patty covered in snow. Under this, a single human ear.

Becoming

IN HIS MORE HOPEFUL MOMENTS, Michaux writes at some length about these things growing in him. Of course he does. He imagines growing within him this great potential for a new city—for a new earth. "Fullwell a childe of the earth," he says, adding the "e" for good measure. He envisions among other things a cancer that grows on other cancers, to draw them off into the newness. The thing eating the other thing like a bladder stepped on so as to cause it to blow up on the other side of the body, growing that way, then stepped on, squashed, collapsing, bulging up, crawling across the body. Cities growing on the remains of cities upon the remains of other cities, building themselves in a blue bottle into which is being spoken a watchword toward the distant tower of Opium Ben.

"But you can't have a diorama of an *idea*, Hershel," Jeffrey once said, the student become the teacher.

But he didn't see Michaux, when he came to the theater that final evening. Michaux—or something like him—that came through the dark and remained just out of sight.

Missive

DEAR JEFFREY, HELLO.
It is 3:17 AM.

Diorama of the Taxidermist

Here, we have a taxidermist in his shop doing taxidermy on a taxidermist who in turn is doing taxidermy on another taxidermist. Three in total, each successive taxidermist being in a greater state of disassembly than the one preceding him.

The fellow who presumably owns the shop is sewing a wig on the second man who is drawing a heap of skin over the mold of the third man, whose foot rests on a log and whose hands are frozen in an odd—an almost cipher—a sigil, because his fishing rod is missing. The skin of the last man lies in folds on the work table. Note the fatty underside. Note as well the presence of a great deal of visceral fat in the abdomen. Perhaps he is a drinker.

Note how the cords stand out on the arms of the man pulling the skin over the mold of his colleague (at such moments there is always someone who will tell you that the skin is the largest of the organs). All round the taxidermist's shop are the preserved specimens of animals which we are meant to assume the last taxidermist has completed. These little creatures appear to be watching the men at their labors.

The paper trail for this undertaking filled seventeen bankers boxes. There was a legal challenge involving one of the family members. If anyone would care to pursue this subject further, I am happy to direct him or her to the pertinent texts. Slide, Jeffrey.

Also note how the animals in the shop are poised upon the very edge of perception, as if they had just heard something, or had perceived someone, watching. Hundreds of little birds, too, litter the shop, deep inside the trees. As if they had just contemplated something in their natural environment and must be *seen* in that subtle act. They are always (and please listen carefully, for this is absolutely vital) to be looking, alert, at something you cannot see. Something, in fact, that cannot be seen. Such was the trick of the art. To imply a separate perception that had been extinguished and placed in the taxidermical mirror.

Diorama of the Loom

Now then. The Diorama of the Loom, shown in the only surviving photograph. A man, at left, in dungarees and workman's cap, disassembles a machine (an industrial loom). His tool satchel. His factoryman's bicycle leans against the railing as he works and so forth. But we go closer, where the scale is much, much different.

For now we see that the loom, in turn, is weaving men within itself, whom themselves assemble industrial looms of the same era, machines which in turn are unweaving other men who are building looms building men disassembling looms. All have their totes and their bicycles. The factories were impossibly large. We really cannot overstate how large the factories were. The workers, especially maintenance personnel, rode bicycles from machine to machine.

In a depiction and a case of industrial madness, this work was a perfect example of what Michaux termed "The Smooth Realm between the godheads and the limit to which they have allowed us to confine them and by which they have doomed us, in retaliation, to defeat." But Michaux may have overstated the case.

Michaux

WE ARE THE EXCEPTION TO the conditions of the museum. The diorama is in this sense aspirational.

Sun Brocade

I HAVE REQUESTED A SENTRY fly, *Musca domestica vigilia*, from the Library of Cancerous Tumors. She is bisected lengthwise, opened like a black lobster. The liquid pooled in the two shells is frozen flat. She has inaugurated a yellow gel within herself, a quiet clear yellow lake upon which the organs lift their complicated islands. Three legs on each of her halves claw at the tray in opposite directions.

The recurrent nerve in this fly—corresponding to our own vagus nerve—has been severed in order to induce cancer in a creature that otherwise does not live long enough for the disease to develop. After, the fly is allowed to move around the lab enclosure, and upon death the cancer is investigated with an eye toward its extinction. In the hand lens, the nerve centers of the fly float their fragile nebula of ropes and clouds buried in the purple murk. And only then do you spot it: a small green cancer attached to the midgut. There is also a foregut cancer as well as a tumor on the insect's salivary gland, devouring toward the black spikelet of its feeding tube.

The sentry fly is known for perching atop flowers or in prominent places in the home. She lays her eggs inside light fixtures where there is a ready supply of insects for the larvae to feed upon. You can train this type of fly to retrieve things. In fact, the sentry fly will retrieve anything it can carry, depositing it in the place provided, then returning to its perch. I myself have placed grains of sand in a light fixture frequented by a fly and observed the individual at work. Crawling over the grains of sand, touching them, she consults her mind. Then she grips one grain close to her body and zips between fixtures, placing the sand in the second one. But it turns out she has been busy on her own project as well. In a third light fixture is the collection of a deep and cryptic nature: grains of ink, a transparent fleck of egg white dried on the stovetop, a panel from the shell of a mechanical insect, an eyelash, sundry petals.

In the hand lens, some sticky substance gums up the grippers of one leg: a blob on the end of the leg, transparent and rose-colored. And outlined clearly as in the ripple of a stained glass is a single strawberry seed, floating within. The seed boiled to death in the sweetness. This is the jam the fly crawled over all those years ago. A final meal, perhaps, or a lure.

Cosmology

IT IS THE NIGHT BEFORE the disaster. The phone rings. Night pigeons burst from the fire escape. I have fallen asleep again, over a book on hand gestures in the plays of the previous century.

With the receiver to my ear, I keep still. No one breathes, not even the lines. I wonder if the caller has hung up. But then a female voice comes from far away, speaking, but I can't make it out.

I consider waking Tom, but it seems unwise.

Meanwhile, moths soften themselves against the windows of the phone. A great pop resounds, and as if something has been freed, the lines regain their usual personality, filling with fuzzes and faint yelps. A shape forms.

The undrawn map of Michaux's numbering system floats in the blackness within. I pinch the corners and pull the glass. The map opens in three dimensions according to yet another change in the system. Some coordinates will necessarily be empty—voids—or partial voids. Michaux located them by way of spherical coordinates as a flotation that could be changed by reference to the angles registered from the origin. A diorama would lie on the arc of a shifting circle with floating angles and would move as if in orbit, relative to all others. The result is a cluttered rectangle made of little loosely connected wooden boxes, with grooves they move in, like an enormous, articulating seamstress's hutch. The boxes are stippled and forested, fish swim inside, cluttered with different-shaped boxes full of little windows, bent-inward canyons of yellow light, seams going into them as they slide within one another, leaking dust and the faint outlines of things inside. Off at the edges float satellite clusters, forested too in tiny boxes, all etched with fine numbers. Flocks of birds fly through the darkness, as black specs that coalesce into numbers.

But I don't believe this. For the animals do not move. They must not move. No, I see now, it is the dioramas that are moving in there. They are drifting. They slide past one another like stately elevators. The windows have confused me. Three, even now, glaze one another in layers. Shifting past. Something moves through the side window of a glass box diorama. They couldn't join up if they tried.

I know in there, beyond those planes of superimposition, I believe, in there is a beginning—the first one he made, fountaining quietly the index he had intended all along, the ur-chart-and-number, done in all naivety as a mistaken hope.

But it's all gone wrong, I admit. No, the number notion—there is no other word for it—is absurd. Utterly useless, the objective correlative strained to absurd fool-ringings and yelps. This is not his fault. How could it be?

Because the diorama is a secret.

That's its job.

And while the soft glasses drift, I spy a diorama alone on its own over a stack of hundreds, one on another, their corners not quite lined up, like a stack of books nudged on accident, and the lone diorama, containing yet another dog flinging its bark with all the energy of its little body, awash, dusting the stars in yellow light like an empty living room, has no link-up, no antecedent whatsoever. It simply came to be. He had intended to fill the gap, I'm certain. But he hadn't done so, and there must have been a purpose to his decision. The number on the bottom of its stranded aquarium—whatever it may be—would otherwise be a severance of doom proportions.

Theater Odeaon: Coda

WIGGINS STOPS.

The earlier feeling is returning. He feels it approaching: that sheen, caused by the theater lights, gives a faint spillage to the air, as of chaff in sunlight, each piece of dust a single fleck of skin like a yellow prism, all spilling down. And the old lecturer peers into this phenomenon, and through the wall he sees to the other side. His heart skips. What he sees he tries to will away. Instead of the audience rising in front of him, there stands a small man facing away and, at the same time, facing towards him, and he feels a second audience, with all its little whispers and shifting sounds, coming into being behind him in the velour. They are rustling their programs. They are touching their hair. And he, Wiggins, the one lecturing from the beginning and now called into question by the little man, resumes speaking while sweat springs under his arms and on his forehead. He hears his voice, but he doesn't know what he's saying. He's caught, they've left him, yet all of them seem to be there, twice, between two instances. Their gaze pours down the back of his neck, he knows no one, this is the attention of strangers. He feels this for the first time: strangers. And the little man, there at the lectern while the dust pours down between the mirror and the light, will not meet his gaze, but whenever Wiggins looks away, the little man looks him full in the eye. This little man is even now in a state of similar pause, it seems to Wiggins. He is frozen, much younger than Wiggins, and then he is the same age, identical to Wiggins, and ill, ill unto death, whereas just before, he had been the picture of health.

He hears himself say, "Doesn't one feel that even the, even the…"

He doesn't know how much time is elapsing. He feels pigeons just off to the side, the blue of pigeons, with their eyes. Circling as if they'd peck at the stage. It's impossible to believe nobody is there. Beats had struck. They were stopped now. Are they finished shelling, then? He has the brief conviction that here in the emptiness is an audience of another kind from some former time and wearing the drapery of the vast distance between here and before, as rags and sagging monstrosities and hollow eyes. And they are tracking him: people from the District of Elsewhere, distinct by virtue of their vagueness, unspooling their bodies from their places of vantage and they are falling over the seats by the century, but he can't see them.

Fingerprints travel over the wall and drift. Green swimmers pass over the surface. Immense drapes pile into folds: this is the folding of the curtain behind the little man, it must be. Wiggins can just see the opera boxes with their gathered valences all in velour and trimmed with cords of a golden thread, running round each of them, toward the stage, and that shocking curtain of the same color (larger than ships' sails, larger than waves in the ocean) some thirty meters tall, heavy like an animal hide turned inside out just skinned, spilling to the very floor, like the tubes of some musical instrument. This curtain seems about to lift with the sound of a shy machine, behind it all. Wiggins closes his eyes. He is still speaking. When he opens his eyes, the little man is still there and makes a gesture of dismissal with a quick sweep of the hand. His lips are moving, but Wiggins hears no sound. There is nothing to do but finish, to get through the evening.

"…even the—as I say—doesn't one feel that the night has a lovely sound? They are all around us.

"Well, they are welcome," he says, not knowing what he means. "And it seems to me that the way to silence is to give no possibility of silence. I am incapable of the silence that would save me. And yet, we're together."

The lamp goes on in the booth, a signal for time from Jeffrey. The lecturer blinks. Has he imagined the light? No, the orange bulb creates itself again up in the booth: a brief wink. Jeffrey is there. And he is signaling.

"It appears we're out of time."

The theater reels, the curtain leans down, and suddenly he is looking at the entire velour rising upward from the back of his head, red and dripping velour. How did he get here.

He is aware of a great commotion, in the direction of his feet, in the audience. A rumbling of feet. Then there is a face, huge as a moon, covering the velour curtain wall. A look of concern floats hugely. The lips are moving, but Wiggins can't hear the voice, which is very far away, indeed. A voice lifts up. There is always, he reflects, some fellow calling stridently for water across a crowd of this kind. And right on cue, there it goes, the call.

A hand reaches for the back of his neck. His chin collapses his trachea for a moment. He struggles. Then the face goes away, replaced by the face he's known for so long: the face of Jeffrey.

His complicated expression hovers over all now. A look of accusation. Of concern. There is hope written there. And weariness. It is all so familiar. Yet he grips Jeffrey's sleeve.

"Come back, Hershel. What did you take?"

"Oh," he hears himself saying, "the usual, Jeffrey. The usual."

VI: RETURNING

Summer Day

OF THOSE EARLY DAYS AFTER moving all of my things and preparing
furiously for the lectures I would no longer give, I spent many days in
the storage basements. Each day, I would go up and leave my attendant
at the elevator. But when I once again emerged in the city at the close
of the day and returned to my apartment, I felt him at the corner of
my eye, going everywhere with me. I would turn my head, expecting
to see him, with his collar bone coming through the suit jacket, but he
wasn't there. And at this time I felt a strange shame, or embarrassment,
that I hadn't—but never mind. Always at the corner of the eye. With
that bullet hole in his cheek. Well, what's to be done.

Throughout the first week, when I would leave the museum after
the long time down, prisoners would be down on their hands and
knees cutting the grass outside the Library. The men were on one side
and the women down on the pedestrian right-of-way, under the street
trees, pulling the grass with their fingers. Further on, the authorities
were putting up barricades for Session IV of the Game of Mote, which
would start in a few days' time. Had the influence of the Mote brought
the prisoners here? Whether perhaps the mote had been placed in *Turf
Grass Management* or perhaps in *Penalogy: Theory and Practice,* I could
only guess. In the roadway horses were pulling the water container
with the broad row of sprinklers at the back to keep down dust. On the
backs of the horses the bodies of flies shone like iridescent scales, but
then I saw it was only the drops of the water spray making a fan of the
air. And the dust was vanishing into the dark carpet of the spray. As if

I were a photograph, I felt that archival impulse to know. That impulse at the heart of the city, with its fall leaves pressed between a billion summer pages in home libraries, each with a Bookend Fraught, and the severed leg of a fawn—naturally, I thought, naturally this impulse was awakened here.

On my final day exploring the storage basements, I had come to an unkempt zone where only skinny bulbs lit the way, high above. The place was almost like a potato barn, cool and musty, where they do the sorting work in low light. Dust covered everything. There were three display cases off to the side, empty. The bottom display case stood on a pallet and two more, willy nilly, on top. One pane had a crack running through it. Nearby, drawered storage boxes on wheels held the effects. Each tooth had been put in a bit of fluff with a little tag on a string: PERSONAL EFFECTS (MASS GRAVES)—SOCIAL ASPECTS. You could open and close the cubbies and poke aside the fluff and see them there. I found a piece of their crockery, those autumnal jars they had used to preserve food. The other things—watches, bracelets and such—were there as well.

And then it came to me. This was Retherford's Display Case project which she had put together with items from the Before Times taken out of the many mass graves that have been discovered over the years. It seems you can't do a public works project without discovering yet another mass grave, four thousand years old, and counting...

I recalled the display cases as they had once been, when I had seen them long ago. There had been buttons made (again) of resin—of every color and shape, lighted from below. They glowed like flowers. And the intricate vertebrae of zippers in several types of metal (brass being the most common, corroded green). Like us, they wore costume jewelry and wristwatches (the innards of which are fascinating—to see how their minds conceived of space, you know). They did etching too; filigrees. I recall a little informational bit about Tynewell's bullet-tracking investigations which showed conclusively that these people were thrown in, many of them, and then shot from above. Tynewell traced no fewer than 3,047 rounds which penetrated, sometimes, six persons before lodging within. Those on the bottom were compressed, and they bore the signs of having fallen from above (wrist and leg fractures, primarily). All repaired, of course. The display case had also contained their glass beads and their coins. The display backlight had made all the things flat, as I recall: calm and two-dimensional. The only thing that remained was that same resin, everything else had decayed (down to dust and beads), and only the grid of the resin weave floated in the display light, never quite able to decay. The grid of a man's shirt.

By way of the basements I had looked into the former world, trying to find the numbers. And as you journey down the well of the aisles, coruscated with boxes rimed in glass, all the while pursuing the visual ring, as if lost in a drain, gone deep into the palace of the dark, you feel the dense suggestions of poisons and tentacular kisses of ideas, ideas, fascinating ideas held down here: the dark star in the throat of a bird.

(And each day, the prisoners were cutting the grass a little bit farther from the Library.)

Michaux

THE DIORAMA'S CHIEF CONTRIBUTION TO the world is silence.

Tom

NEXT MORNING, ELBOWS ON KNEES and looking up at me through the railing of the balcony, Tom tells me that news of his wife's death had come by phone two years before. Now, at night he makes note of the telephone pole numbers. Only the poles with streetlights attached to them have numbers, he says. All others are blank—with only the code for the species of tree burned into their cylinders—carrying the lines to their points of departure. He has begun to map them on his walks and says, as to probability, they are "non-sequential," as if in spite of their arrangement, they are all—together at once—in a wood that has been unwound from a spool as a single line of trees in an endless sidewalk with black pools between. So, finding no rational way to tie the numbers into his investigations, he says he's hit a cold spot with the game of Mote. Nothing seems to be working the past several days, as if "the world has changed."

I understand what he means. All of what I had seen suddenly left me, and I thought to myself, where was that origin point, that blue-black cube, ur-cold and enduring, from which the news of a beginning would arrive?

Mote

TOM MAY BE RESPONDING TO the influence of the mote itself. The summer game, after all, is well underway. The movements and counter-movements have bent the shape of things. I recall an internship I once had while at the Farmers College helping an old man—somewhat famous in his day and now a grim, sprung-hipped emeritus with his hair sticking up—prepare his mote strategy for a game that was to begin the following season. He was known in the game for his ruthlessness, this man, and his clever cloaking maneuvers. But now his mouth, when he thought you weren't looking, fell kind of slack and wet.

There were several of us students gnashing ourselves with anxiety, running up and down the empty library. We were dealing at the time with live-play: brief instances of strategy where a real mote is used under controlled conditions. As a result, we had a real mote in our possession, shut up in a box. I recall reaching for the case with the thing inside it in response to some directive howled at me by that skinny old man. In hurrying to respond, the wooden case opened in my hands, sort of slipped, and I saw inside a tiny speck in blue velvet—blue as the sky, but cold—twinkling in the box. I felt it on my face: that tensile shard becoming suddenly aware of me.

Against my cheek a thermal billow swept. It was not quite coolness, not quite heat. I can only say it was not magnetism but that it felt like magnetism looks, to the eye. The way objects smarten up in the presence of the magnet, and swivel, and rush inward. It is like static electricity against your skin, only that doesn't quite express it, either.

All I can say is you feel it, especially when the box is fully opened and even more so when the mote is lifted out with tweezers—you feel it move your hair. Your sweater buzzes with static, too, down the back of your neck, shifting the lint for meters around. But you see, your hair hasn't moved because nothing moves in the early presence of the mote. It is only later, when time has lengthened, that things begin to move. And even then, only far away from the venue.

I believe this is happening to Tom. The mote has found him.

Amateur

A WALL OF HUMIDITY ENVELOPES the city. I have been trying for errands, one each day. Now, I hurry home for lunch, and when I arrive, I see that the left eye has fallen out of my finch. A red bead, it lies next to the nut she had been about to peck. The socket has a puckered look, and I can see the white cotton stuffing. After lunch I begin to disassemble the cases. It is full night when I have them apart. In the light of the lamp I tweeze the eye and put it in a dish for tomorrow.

Something thumps in the wall—perhaps Carla hanging a picture. A faint screech comes from the direction of the balcony. Perhaps an owl or swing set chains hoisting some exiled teenager.

Rabbit skin glue is very powerful, but it is possible to rely too much on it. Before I go to bed, I'll research changing the formulation.

Amateur

ON SECOND THOUGHT I AM reluctant to put the theen finch diorama back together. There are, I feel, key decisions that still have to be made. On close examination, for example, the legs of the storebought male have an undue shine; you see them and think, "Metal." Perhaps I can introduce the dryness you often see on birds' legs, that reptilian scaling. Or I can band the male with an aluminum number and ask Tom for advice on the grammar of band numbers. Or I could redo the backdrop, from black to a continuation of the forest floor, going out and out, disappearing in the simple distance.

Above all, I have to be careful. Things have a way of getting out of hand. When you look at dioramas where this has happened, you can glimpse someone inside the space. They've gotten in the way. The animals have become props. For the story, you know. Yet I am the first to admit the animal has to be doing something. It can't just be standing there, for then it would be mere taxidermy, a sort of hunting trophy. What the animal does must be its own idea, not what it would have done but what it intends to do, on its own, as a matter of survival.

Amateur

I HAVE IT. I'LL PUT two trillium in the diorama, one in full bloom, the other just about to emerge in the quiet woods, pushing up the loam. I can make them out of paper dyed with careful gradations of green ink. This will take attention away from the metal legs of the male finch, which if I'm honest, I lack the skill to paint to begin with. I tell Carla, whom I've kept updated on my progress.

"I hate to be the one to break it to you, Wiggins," she says, "but isn't trillium a spring flower—or early summer? You have hazelnuts. That says fall."

She's right, of course. The seasons can't be accidental, no matter what might change on its own. Nevertheless, I'm reluctant to capitulate. The hazelnuts could be from the season before.

But Carla isn't convinced.

Alive

I FIND MYSELF ALWAYS ON the lookout for dead animals now.

In the roadway when I'm on the trolley: to what degree is that squirrel crushed? Might it be salvageable? In the park: a pile of feathers from some owl's night meal. The geese in the sky: which one of them might be flagging?

It's probably inevitable, therefore, that word got out, and people from the retirement block began to tell me about dead animals they had seen while going about their day. Twice, people have brought me carcasses. The woman on the top floor arrived the other day with a baby woodchuck in a box. Then Tom presented me with a rat he'd discovered near the river.

Mind you, I am grateful. I had every intention of using them. I sketched hasty plans. The rat was to be on its hind legs, nose lifted, scenting the air for an unseen danger. I needn't have done anything else because the viewer was to have done the rest. The woodchuck I'd wanted to display on the ground, minding its own business, eating clover as if it had all the time in the world.

I wasn't fast enough. They began to rot. So in the early morning I took them to our building's compost and scooped out a place and put them in.

Amber

AMBER WAS THE FIRST DIORAMA. Smelling of pine. We claimed them by way of our future eye. The prism of fancy begins and ends here.

I have often wondered, however, if the geode and its hidden cities is where all this began. A place you could never go, made for you alone.

As when we go to sleep, the sense that life has ended. And now that life has ended, and we've fantasized ourselves out of the world, the fear is less continuous, if you see what I mean. There are gaps in the fabric. We're built this way, as some sort of grace enters in. One doesn't precisely *trust* it, mind you. But there it is: we absolutely must be gone. But then, a new day comes...

One Diorama

Need we go on?

Because somewhere it has been written that if one has seen a single diorama, the imagination builds the rest. All dioramas flower from the first sight. This is because the diorama, as an idea, as a place, as a set of gestures, is a single entity and a law of "nature." The phenomena are forever the same.

And so there is but one diorama, just as, although many kinds of birds fly together from one place under the trees to some other place, there is but one flock, singular. A diorama goes on and on within itself.

Outward-facing, this phenomenon of display (with no indwelling reality) grows collective in the hallway's arrangement, growing into a new structure of time, as the beginning of a new species.

The beginning of a new species.

I knew it was there, but I couldn't find it.

Goll found it.

The Mind of the Next World waits within ourselves. All that high tremble to the City is gone now in the near dark of the apartment. The rain falls elsewhere, and then one feels the Mind of the Next World come close. But the rain has originated in the diorama where the wind brings the scent of another rain far off, and so the moment of our observation has paused, and entered history.

book ii: people

In Vantage

THE PASSENGER PIGEONS BEGIN THEIR migration: a tugging, a yearning. They lift in the forest, then settle. Snow drips from thawing trees. The lymph rises.

One bird, with only one eye, is the first to jump. All at once, below her a roar opens over the forest, and the birds begin to fly. They cross the dimensions. They overfly different worlds. Below, all the trees have been cut, and the stumps are yellow circles. Then the ground warps, stretches. Those same stumps are trees. The birds land for the night, pecking new buds. They crank their necks. The next day, they roar up again and fly. Over a ruined city. Just now, the city is whole. Then buildings of glass turn to timber frames, shrinking; then, when the passenger pigeons cross another world, the buildings warp again into surprising cubes. The cubes shrivel, and the outwash plain on which the cities were built spreads a broad delta, cut with runnels.

Among the living birds the dead fly, too. Their bodies tatter, but they fly on, eyeless, following their young, those they made. Sometimes, their outlines grow faint across the sky. They become invisible, but the pigeon with one eye can feel them all around, following in a vaporous mass.

Hawks, eagles prey on the birds. Now, there are no passenger pigeons, but only for a single moment. In the billions they become a vapor, a giant wind of invisible feathers. And when the wind crosses into another world, the birds are there again, flying with the living and the dead. The pigeon with one eye drafts behind other birds. In the middle of the flock they seem to float without effort, pulled along by the migration whose slipstream is miles and miles wide. She flies toward the old man.

**

He felt the breeze change a week ago when the trades shifted on a dial. The old man feeds the fire, and a spring rain squalls, drawing cold over the buildings. He washes his hands to warm them. The fire is a pretty orange.

The first birds arrive in the city. Like flapping paper sacks, they land and shuffle themselves open and closed. More birds come. A guidebook on the table reads, "Passenger pigeons are the most numerous animal in the world and always will be." In their billions they set way together. This is only the beginning of the migration.

To keep his circulation running, the old man stands at the railing looking down at the farms on the tops of the buildings. Pumpkin vines. Espaliered plum and apple orchards. Off to the left, the building made entirely of beehives and with a processing plant underneath, and bee keepers on rope and swing inspect the hives like window washers, their smokers puffing. On the top of another building far below, a girl is fishing in the pond, oval-shaped and rimed in green gore. The water depth can be seen, like the lines on topographical maps, darkening toward the center.

Every year, the old man waits for the one-eyed bird and she always comes, landing shyly, to peck at the seeds in the outstretched tin.

Days and days pass. The one-eyed pigeon drifts in and out of memory, deep memory and more specific memory. She is flying over the forests and swampland. Sometimes she can't see the ground the flock is so thick. Wishing sounds of wings and bird cries. She adds her voice. The sun is setting. The flock skims the trees, which pull the pigeons down until all have roosted. The next morning, in heaving roars, the flock resumes flight. Three round barns pass below. Then the flock passes an infantry division marching on the high road. In the distance skyscrapers spike the sky, then are disappeared. What is one bird when compared to a system of billions moving in the sky. Wait for one bird. Plenum and vacuum. They flow over the chestnut forests in bloom, the odor of the seed of men. Frogs sing in vernal pools. The one-eyed bird, her memory comes like a river, flows through her and is forgotten. She inhales the scents of her previous crossings. Impossibly familiar, around her are birds she has known, and most are strangers that she must have known at some time.

On the morning the first birds arrive in the City, the old man stands at the railing. The wind burns his fresh-shaven cheeks. To the east the sky blackens. He hears a rumbling sound. Then the first wave of birds is upon the city. In a long sine they pass overhead. The old man opens his pocket watch, whose radium dial can be seen in the shadow. Still the birds pass. Five minutes. Six minutes of darkness. He remains under the overhang as the droppings fall on a slant. Ten minutes. Twelve. Only then does the flock thin and the air grow light.

And there she is.

She pecks in the pan. Jerking, with a wary tip to her head. And that glazed eye, the blind threaded with purple lines. The bird with one eye bursts upward, scattering the seed in the pan, and lands on his arm.

"Well hello, lady."

All around, the pigeons cross the sky, and the lady pigeon feels them flow by, great mass of pigeon-smelling feathers and droppings.

Impassive, she jerks her head, tipping her skull, the purpled-over eye shuttered through with cracks. Metal gleams under her feathers.

"Where have you been? All these times…"

The bird lets him stroke her neck.

"The forest…"

The sky grows dark again. The second wave of birds has arrived. Thirteen minutes, and she's gone, she's joined them to go over the Channel, where a war is on.

The Town

THE TELEPHONE RINGS. CLICKS CRACKLE through the night lines. Out of the smoke, a voice identifies itself as a representative of the museum. The voice is giving me instructions. I fumble for a pen.

I have been petitioning for years to visit the Diorama of the Town, and my summons has finally come. I am given two days to report to the sheds for the ten-day journey.

In the interim I run around frantically getting the things I will need. Tom loans me a suitcase to which I add my own small valise, and lay things out on the bed, and make decisions. I am not a traveler by nature. I wonder if the museum knows this.

I feel almost giddy.

The Town is a Geographical Diorama. Its tremendous expanse (the topography, the depiction of weather, et cetera) gives the category its name. I had sought to visit the exhibit for decades when my health was more robust, but alas, the acceptance and admission process was (in my case) long.

In your petition to visit the Town you must give your reasons, scholarly or otherwise, for wishing to trespass on the undeniably fragile ground. Perhaps you are a scholar of architecture, a taxidermical biologist searching for samples of a rare animal or of an extinct human community, which can be found only there. Over time, my reasons for visiting have changed. Originally, I had hoped to find examples of the display of the lone worker, separated from community, and had looked forward to whatever form these researches would take in the hopes they would cast light upon my own quest for answers regarding the nature of the relationship between Michaux and Goll. But the museum seldom answers questions.

That night, as I hang up the phone, spring snow is turning to rain and falling on the leaves. I look at all the volumes in my library lined up as a wall, and I think to myself, "So this is their game."

Carla

I know immediately I must speak to Carla, since she worked in the Town for years. I have brought a bottle of wine.

"So you're going, are you? Well well well."

There is a gloss and a sleepy irony to her eye. Carla drinks perhaps too much wine, as Tom drinks too much whiskey. Sitting on her balcony overlooking the water tank across the way, I ask her what to expect.

Her face assumes a thoughtful expression. I see that she has gone somewhere else.

"Well, it's very quiet," she says.

I take a sip of wine, mindful of what it will do to my stomach.

"I knew a man," Carla adds, "a sensitive man (not that you're sensitive, but you see what I mean)—he was a draper. He was there for two weeks, and he lost his mind—went a little crazy. He had to be reassigned."

What should I look out for, what should I pay attention to, especially?

"Oh my," Carla says, laughing. "You are far gone, aren't you?"

I insist that my interest is of a scholarly nature and that I am—first and foremost—a scholar.

"Aren't we all," Carla says flatly.

I feel my face growing warm.

She holds up a placating hand. "Okay. All right." She takes a breath and looks down for a moment. She's gone to that earlier place again. She seems to be deciding something. Something about the Town. Then she shakes her head. There's a sad expression on her face.

"Unfortunately, Wiggins, there's something there for everyone."

Itinerary

THE TRAIN JOURNEY WILL TAKE ten days. We will stop along the way at preapproved locations. I am to be accompanied by an assistant docent who will answer questions and ensure compliance with the rules. I am to touch nothing. I am to go nowhere unaccompanied. To step outside this mandate is to abort the tour immediately. There will be considerable walking. I pack my cane. After having applied and petitioned so long, I cannot imagine having some difficulty along the way.

As I am leaving the apartment, Tom appears in the hallway. He reaches down and buckles a buckle I've left undone. He pats me on the shoulder. "Don't let it get to you too much."

My guide, Mr. Emery, meets me in the entrance lobby of the sheds. He is a distant little man, very professional, of about twenty-five years of age. He has a small, yet upright stillness about him. He is the sort of person who had been taught from an early age to meet the world with good posture and who had taken the lesson rather too close to heart. I think him absurd as he stands there twitching, not sure whether to smile or smooth his pockets.

There is something endearing, however, about such a flaw, for after all, doesn't it strike back into just that hidden lesson (learned probably from an uncle or a stentorian grandmother) that formed the picture of his childhood? One can only guess, of course. But I have the feeling this isn't far from the truth: some rule of presentation had been meant to set one up smartly in the face of the world and be a kind of bulwark against an ongoing collapse. He wears his immediate history, his family always with him as ghosts.

All of his gestures end before they begin. He is always holding back, embarrassed. Yet you feel him judging you. Half-smiling, always hiding. Before speaking, he will pause, a small smile, somewhat timid and yet not altogether unsly, forming at the corner of his mouth, before the words follow. At these times he seems eminently aware that he is about to speak and cognizant equally of the novelty of speech. Perhaps he spends too much time alone. I cannot put my finger on it, but I want to help him along. He seems fearful, for my sake, I guess at the imagined quiet at the heart of my, an older person's, experience of the world. Whenever I ask him a question, he seems to be turning over several lessons that had been imparted to him during some obscure occupational training and pleased to put the evasion to use in the real world. I suspect that he had been chosen not for his expertise but for his ignorance.

We are to travel the Sectors and Wards with which Mr. Emery is familiar. He calls it his "route." The rest of the Town, stretching far and wide, he doesn't know, but he is "getting certified." I gather that Mr. Emery's regular duties are in the capacity of an inspector who checks on the welfare of the place. Leaks, lights out, this sort of thing. In short, any change that may have come about in the interim of his last travels, it is his duty to report. He has made this journey, five days out, five back, many times. There will be little inns along the way, stranded, simple resting places that had been part of an earlier plan to accommodate visitors. A skeleton staff will see to our needs.

As I say, he is about twenty-five, short in stature. He has the upright carriage, something in the angle of the chin, of men, like myself, who aspire to tallness, as if they are always looking over the top of something. I ask him about his family. He is reticent, as if they are a source of some concern. He had, he says, a sister. She had worked on a farm in the city. What part of the city is he from? "I'm from many places, sir."

Emery

THERE IS A FALSE RETICENCE about him. I don't know if I've said that. He wants to speak. You can feel him making calculations about what he can, and cannot, say. As if, were he to get talking, he wouldn't be able to control what he said. He watches you when he speaks, watches for some clue as to how things are landing, so that he will know what not to say next. He peers too deeply into your face. He is seeking permission: all the permissions of what might be said, were he able. The suitcoat—and the museum tie—lock him in. They are glued to his frame. I had met with plenty of similar men and women in my department. They kept to themselves, every one of them. You were always wondering what they were thinking. They were easy objects of scorn, and jokes. They thought they could get by on their work alone, done in privacy. Their lack of an opinion about the Town became, to us, the very image of their hidden opinion, and so we didn't trust them. Yet when you got to know them, you saw that they, of all people, had the most active inner worlds and the strangest, most astonishing opinions.

Goll

BUT A BIT ABOUT MINISTER Goll, that man of endless opinions. He was born into a sort of half-privilege in the outskirts of the city. Little is known of his early life. It is said his mother ran a successful factory for the restoration of furniture—peeling chairs, separating legs and backs, and putting them back together, restained and waxed, till they appeared newly old. The company prospered and expanded.

As a child Goll did not take to the lesser private school he was doomed to attend. He would later rail against the prestigious academies and claim they were soft. He preferred physical contests, in teams, with himself as the captain. He claims to have been especially accomplished at the throwing of wooden disks. In fact, Goll drew most of his political lessons from sport. He saw himself as above the children of old wealth, because his family claimed to have built its empire "from nothing," and thus he retained the fighting spirit they had lost.

He was a great imitator; he imagined the lives of the established families—their buildings, their decorations, their manners—and set himself up in parallel as a better version, more authentic than they, purer. Strangely, he claims not to have known his parents, who had been consumed by business matters and left him to fend for himself, aided of course by a small army of pinched nurses, despairing tutors, and instructors in guns, marching, climbing, fishing, and whatever else the boy took a fancy to.

"Your family are strangers," he said by way of a general law, extempore. "They are versions of yourself that you have gone beyond."

When he took over the family factories, the furniture became needlessly elaborate, glistening, glowing and bulbous. In a matter of years he bankrupted those divisions of the firm he'd been allowed to manage, which he blamed on laws privileging the competition. At this time he went into politics, on a platform of change, winning the seat when his opponent mysteriously withdrew.

Goll wanted to alter the city, he said, so that it reflected the destiny of the people within. His speechwriter put it this way: "Geography, in the totality of its mandate, is permission."

Goll fired her on the spot.

In parliament his efforts to raise himself failed, and he was relegated to a few, minor administrative chairmanships, among them the Assistant to the Ministry of Culture. In time he maneuvered himself into the top post, mostly on the strength of his fundraising, but he was forced to resign after a scandal involving upholstery contracts and the laundering of money through charitable organizations. But Goll moved too fast for scandal, so fast in fact that his image, as in a photograph of a speeding carriage, blurred into new forms. Everyone knew his origins, but he began to claim other birthrights, other origins. Aligning himself with the workers, he claimed to have been one of them, had risen from the factory floor to the chairmanship and had always had his workers' interests in mind. He said he had once been a scientist, too, but that the discipline was too "pinched" for an enterprising man. He claimed that a process—be it learning, business, or love—if it is to be great at all, can always be felt, in the gut, right before your eyes, as an image of the future.

Intending to shape that future and hoping to sell some of his family's land that had escaped the creditors, he set his sights on the city's planning department. He imagined "great, green bulwarks, great arboricious walls," by which he meant parks. Forests, great rivers, black icy streams that bent into mysterious regions where one could test oneself against nature; bridges that would appear out of nowhere and emerge a thousand feet off the ground, to the astonishment of workers in the skyscrapers. Rivers of commerce. And fisheries. And endless stocks of game. The audacity of this vision attracted backers and at first gained momentum, but again Goll was exiled into what he felt was a minor committee chairmanship, in the Department of Museums. As war broke out in the city, Goll took advantage of the chaos to consolidate power. The rest is well known. In spite of his rise, however, and his taking over of the government, he maintained control of the Department of Museums. He saw a certain flexibility in museums. They were, after all, what you claimed them to be, and they were stocked with whatever you wished, things you wanted to put aside, things you must value.

He commissioned museums and libraries (which he said were "a type of museum") on every pattern, dashing off ideas from the fireside. What might be done with a library of radios, for example? Or a library of maps containing things that should be there, rather than things that are? And what about a library of faces, where you could check out wooden masks—for festivals, parties, and so forth—or plasticine things like noses, teeth, and mustaches made of resin, or period clothing. Now there was a thing they were always trying to get rid of: the past, the clothing of the past, when they knew how to make things.

And why not a museum of the industrial methods for the production of these things? To bring back the factories as they had once been, without all the ease, where you had to be on your toes. A museum for the production *of all things*, for which machines had once been designed, machines that could be used for nothing else, and now were in danger of disappearing: a museum of endangered machines.

Underlings ran around, frantic. Architects drew plans. Goll broke ground with ceremonial shovels and museums rose, and strange libraries. One evening he conceived the Museum of Museums, to the despair of the architects, who designed a vast model train set I had seen as a boy, in preparation for the real thing: an enormous block of a building with moving engines and rails set into the street to hoist, floor on floor, old museums that had been taken from the city and stored whole—in case they would be needed—"for the edification, for all posterity," according to his speechwriter.

Both men, Michaux and Goll, had lived during times when it was possible to imagine the world. The two were distant in time, but I imagined Michaux on a building top, doing semaphores across the winter canopy. The flags snap into place. Through the snow, Goll, in another building a mile away, is riding the elevator up, getting closer to his vision.

The Game Room of Minister Goll

IT IS SAID GOLL BEGAN as a hobbyist. These early specimens he put into a trophy room. Heads, antlers: that which he'd gotten while hunting. Like many wealthy people who become interested in a thing, he soon committed more resources. And then he became obsessed. Taxidermy grew into dioramicism. The exiled heads on their mountings grew bodies. Shy foliage began to sprout, little shrubs, rock outcroppings, and the backdrop painted with skill. He expanded the Game Room many times. To display them, he kept having new buildings designed, built, then scrapped because his hunting expeditions (often of made-up animals) overwhelmed the capacity of the rooms. Fed up with the limitations of traditional trophy rooms, he decided to solve the size problem once and for all.

Goll was a notoriously avid hunter. No game was too small. Meanwhile, children adored him. He always had a little toy in his coat pocket, some small trinket of a clown or a bird, and the Game Room was his first foray into the large-scale diorama, blooming to over nine hundred acres of alcoves and inset dioramas surrounding larger expanses in which no detail is out of place. All is covered in glass sheets with various pathways and clifflike platforms for viewing. Every animal he had killed himself; this was a point of pride. He wanted a place you could get lost in, even if you knew the way.

At the height of his adventures, a staff of five hundred taxidermists occupied the dormitory adjoining the workshops. Goll was always on one expedition or another. He hunted an entire herd of caribou on one weekend, felling them with a machine gun. Here they are, running over the icy river. Their nostrils flare, the antlers laid back. Goll is said to have carried the gun himself.

He captured these green ibis with nets. There are over one thousand birds in the marsh. Each bird, each beast, I can assure you, is real. Goll insisted there would be no mockups. The financing for this project, as for the Town, was done in the usual way. Through sheer personality and guile during a time of exquisite profligacy, of shining halls and balusters, shocking levels of wealth that have become, of course, quaint in our time, the funds were gotten. There are even preserved human specimens, with their binoculars and scopes, "soft" observers of the living world, fixing their field-glasses on the animals.

Because Minister Goll also hunted people. Each one of his human trophies once had a sort of dossier and also a plaque explaining matters. Goll claimed to have kept records in order to preserve an essential dignity in the subjects. But I think it more likely that he feared our disbelief; he must fight claims that the figures had been faked, as in a wax museum. Subsequently, Goll had these dossiers and records destroyed, along with bills of lading and purchase orders for materials. Journals. Photographs. Some essential anxiety led to this decision, I think. Verification—that which comes after—when we have lost control of the project, is the main danger.

The museum looks this problem in the eye. Critics have held that the museum is perhaps too proud of the fact. But no matter. A museum is in the business of truth, with respect to itself. Perhaps *only* in respect to itself. The museum itself is the only exhibit in the end. The Diorama of the Town makes these early hobby rooms seem quite quaint.

Herald

We have only fifteen minutes to see Goll's other hobby diorama, The *Herald* Building, which is situated next to the Game Room.

This building of fifteen stories, enameled brick, with a great Herald sign atop, at night in neon of red and lime, is a true wonder. Before Goll could be stopped, he surrounded the original *Herald* Building, full of workers and people going about their day. Here, we have workers at the presses. In the lobby a male receptionist with a balletic posture. Even the carpets have been specially woven, all the woodwork planed like caramel, and the old, iron press machine displayed prominently as you enter. In the basement stands the modern press, still capable of printing, with its yellow paint and safety rails and the great rolls of paper yellowing to vinegar. Goll even preserved the woman filling the ink tanks from a horse-drawn barrel. The taxidermy is of the highest quality. The ink pipe enters a valve set into the pavement outside the building.

Goll put to death everyone he found there. The reason? He had been angered by an editorial cartoon. Then, after removing all of the deceased, he put the entire building to flame.

Goll had a very firm opinion on the matter of preservation. To display a building with its shrubs and benches out front, its flags and pediment, a building that already existed, and furthermore, to disassemble the structure and move it and reassemble it elsewhere, was to engage in a lie, and Minister Goll hated lies of this kind. A laziness, is how he often put it. The thing must be destroyed, then built again, exactly as it had been, on new terms. Every fixture and tap must function as designed, but—and this is the key—*must never again have the need.* Otherwise, all you were doing was removing people, weatherproofing the place and then putting them back inside. Goll wished for a private *Herald* building, bustling with silences. He wanted no artifact. Give him the thing itself, made new.

The Journey

WE ARE FORTUNATE TO CATCH an electric tram to Station White, a little putt-putt car which Mr. Emery operates himself, pulling a great trolley, like an insect head with a giant body. The dry roads creep by at a stately pace, then faster in the straight courses. Our passage causes the tie of one man to flutter and settle on his shoulder. I wonder if someone will come by and lay it flat.

Station White, from which we will depart for the Interior, is as large as that station in our own city. Men stand around. Indoor pigeons. The great ceiling arches, all glass, toward the "sky." Birds stand on the surface of the station. They never move. Above, the enormous ceiling of the sheds looms. Even a few droppings-streaks for effect are painted on the station glass as if it has lately seen rain. Meanwhile, the train waits, with a burden of heat. She is an up-to-date diesel model, outfitted to do steam, painted orange and enameled in places with lines of red. There is always something parental about a train. She pulls seven Pullman cars, five of which are dioramic displays, the sixth for crew. The seventh I have to myself, with Emery at the other end, and from the platform I can see the figures in the other cars, travelers from some earlier period: men and women busy, fussing; a man with a newspaper, stiff with starch; a woman seeing to little details, hanging something on a rod over her head. None of them move.

We find our coach. I am shown to a luxurious little cubby of a room with all sorts of curlicues and outfittings and upholsteries. Mr.

Emery helps me with my luggage in the shy way that younger men have, a kind of holding back as they attempt to heave a heavy object while maintaining courtesy. An attendant brings me a seltzer to which I add a small libation of my own. After a short while the train comes against its couplers with a jerk. I feel my heart quicken. We roll into a tunnel, and the station is gone. The little ceiling lamp, from some other era, begins to sway and, as the train makes clasping and unbuckling sounds, growing faster and more frantic, my shoulder is thrown against the cushion. When we come out of the tunnel, the landscape has been rendered wet, as if it were raining. All the people stand waiting under the black shells of their umbrellas.

Next thing I know, the land has opened to the "rain." We are rushing through an interim scene, half country, half city. There are old-fashioned farms. I distinctly see a woman frozen, turning a compost pile with a pitchfork while pigs watch. Then she is gone. That fast. My eye hungers after the scenes that will make stories, but there are too many. At one rail crossing there is a carriage crash, rendered fully. Two farmers are arguing, a broken axle, the hayload spilled over the road. Hills move in the distance. Near objects move the opposite direction, slipping past one another.

Subsequent demands to open the Diorama of the Town to the public were, and always have been, met with paeans to respect and dignity. "Let the dead rest." In addition, calls to dismantle the entire project and to give the victims a proper burial have run up against a lack of names. The hope was, and remains, that the vast real estate could be put to excellent use. But who would wish to live there?

I try, and fail, to gain a response from Mr. Emery on this matter. Going down the aisle of the car, I find him in a sleeper smaller than my own. He regards me quietly for a moment too long, his mouth forming shapes not quite sly, not quite humorous as he shifts through a host of possible responses.

"No signs of a change on the horizon, sir," he says. He seems pleased to be able to tell me this. And the question is closed. But his expression says he is leaving something out.

Sometime later, the train slows. There is a knock at the compartment door. Mr. Emery, putting his head in, says, "First stop, sir."

I am surprised. We have only been traveling a short time. Minutes, I feel. I go to the closet for my raincoat before I remember the rain isn't real.

Levels

LEAVING THE TRAIN, WE WALK until the shopfronts end and the sky opens to a sort of moorland. I crane my neck. Above, the surface of the shed-roof looks like sky, expertly concealed. We come to the little cottage among many other dwellings made of stone, dotting the countryside, far away. Glossy piles of fresh-cut peat near every one. A shepherd stands stiff as a board near a dog. Smoke is frozen above the hut's stovepipe.

The cottage itself is set in a garden that never grows and never sheds a bloom but one in which the species are all appropriate to the climate. Inside this little house—which is of real stone—there sits a man at a small repast. He is middle-aged. His hands are dirty. We are given to understand he is the husband. He lifts a soup spoon to his mustache, poised there midslurp. In the bowl of the spoon one can discern individual vegetables in a clear broth. The butter has just begun to melt on his bread, a single slice resting directly on the tabletop.

Each room of the house has received such care. In one a little girl doing a puzzle, alone. A woman, presumably the mother, knitting upstairs in front of a peat fire. Why none eats with the man goes unexplained. The Diorama of the Town, Emery explains, is a secret place, full of stories you have to figure out. One cottage over, two children in tiny white dresses totter like chickens around the yard. And the girl in the rear garden, the oldest of the family, with her foot on a red ball, prompt in waiting.

We board the train.

"Is every cottage so done up?" I ask.

"Every one, sir," Emery says. "Next stop in one hour."

Eric Polle

BACK IN THE TRAIN COMPARTMENT, I try to mark everything, every detail. Soon, I fall back. I close my eyes. I am thinking of the lobby at the entrance of the Town and of the strange man who had been sitting there. He had been a worker in the Town of a very unique sort; I had intended, as part of my earlier proposal to visit the Town, to make him the focus of my investigations. I have brought along an old catalogue of the Town, the kind they used to sell in the souvenir shop. Now, I turn the pages and soon find the photograph I've been searching for. There, on the facing page, is Eric Polle on his bench, staring glassily out.

Polle had been the custodian in the early days of the Town. He had been responsible for the upkeep of the lobby all those years ago. He is part of the Town exhibit now, but he was once positioned outside as if he were one of us, waiting on his bench to go inside. The exhibit glass, which had once been behind him, has since been extended to include him. Mary Retherford was commissioned for the remodel. It was she who brought the glass to Polle and made it swoop round him like a bubble. This was done to set him and his great crime apart.

In the lobby Polle is unscrewing the lid of his coffee container. He is taking a break from the museum, he is resting, he is getting ready to return to the exhibits. Looking up, he greets us with a pleasant expression. Some "necessary neutrality" plays around the glassy corners of his mouth, smooths his cheeks, parts his hair.

The Town and the Man

As I say, by design before you cross over to board your train for the Interior, you pass by Eric Polle and the explanatory matter, positioned on slanted boards. The exhibit explains Eric Polle's role in the early business of the Town. He was a bachelor who wrote to his mother about his work life and what was going on in the Town and a little bit about its history. Though reticent by nature with his fellow workers, Eric Polle by no means held back when addressing his only friend, who had raised him to be conscientious and agreeable. And he missed very little of the goings-on in those early days: the placement of human beings, the size of the exhibit and the plans for its expansion, secrecy in plain view. That Minister Goll was using the Town to disappear—and then display—his enemies. The whole story with which we have become familiar was first apprehended by Polle, who remained silent and, along with his mother, did nothing.

The museum catalog reproduces one of his letters in a sidebar. Odd penmanship. And here he is with his coffee container, dressed as a gentlemen of a hundred years ago, in tweeds. Pulled outward by the Retherford glass, he wears shoes that you imagine creak pleasantly. An umbrella. Note the gesture of the left hand. The poise of the fingertips on the coffee cylinder, as if to unscrew the cap. Polle is making, has been caused to make, a sign. Scholars have traced this sign—pinky finger poised, thumb and middle finger making contact with the cap—to the Sigil of Welcome that ladies would give, with an ironic twist to the mouth, to individuals they in actuality despised. The gesture comes directly from partisans of Minister Goll, who would flash it in the streets, and who later maintained control of the Town even after the Minister's downfall. Eric Polle's placement was part of that effort to educate the public.

The choice to keep the Polle exhibit whole is of note. The only way to reverse Polle's gesture, it was felt, was to encase him, too, in glass.

Put Polle at the entrance? Goll's supporters said in response. Very well. But to us, he is a hero, the symbol of calm. Careful inspection shows that, after the placement of the glass, Polle's hand had been cut off, and replaced with the cap gesture.

The problem is, you don't know what he is thinking, Polle. What the symbols mean to him, given all he knows. I peer at his picture in the catalogue. And yet, you do know what he is thinking. Because you know. He is told they deserve their fate, no doubt. That is enough for him. For Polle the Town has entered the kaleidoscope: it is an exception to the rule. The permission has already been granted. Once granted, it is simply "natural." A natural flow from one place to another. Opium Ben, the poet has it, "pours his monaural liquid over the City."

Polle is off the hook. He can rest easy.

Perhaps he is thinking nothing.

Sigil in Tweed

BUT EFFORTS TO MANIPULATE POLLE'S gesture do not end there. At the elbow of his jacket, in the tweed itself, is a message. The close-up in the catalogue reveals a sort of code woven into the fabric. This is one of the many examples of how the designers of such dioramas, and especially in scenes containing human beings, have placed their mark on the dead. But there is a second method, far stranger (and of which Eric Polle is the first exemplar).

We refer to the posing of the dead. Some gesture—of the hand, or the whole body—will be altered toward some other object in the diorama. The finger positions or the direction of the specimen's gaze will be positioned toward a clue that is hidden in the scene. This is in part why the eyelines often seem subtly askew in dioramas.

The expression of that child in the cottage, utterly empty. Note the shape of the four-cornered hatchmarks burned into the wood of the mantle to which the child's face has been turned. There we find a second symbol often found in the homes of partisans.

In another example, by way of the wife figure in this kitchen, whose down-directed eye alerts us to the arrangement of freckles on the husband's arm, we find the same, four-cornered sigil. Smithe refers offhand to the belief that it is the souls of the people in dioramas, the ghost souls of the murdered coming back, that etch the messages into such scenes. Their purpose was to "speak their erasure," which they would do by "an act of will." But this seems too optimistic.

Restoration

SEVERAL DECADES AGO, THE TAXIDERMY of Eric Polle began to fail. Note the hair has begun to fall out, the work of a fungus that thrives in the bright light and dry air of the diorama. *Enblancas foetida.* The skin lightens with a white mold that takes years to thicken on the face and all the while has been spreading under the clothing. Only an archival photograph, happened on by chance during another project, alerted the conservator.

They unpin Polle from the bench. There is a discoloration to the wood where his buttocks have rested for nearly two hundred years.

In the workshop, the identification of the spore. The proper fungicide administered. After a series of wettings and dryings undertaken to confuse the moldlike growth and drive it out, a final drying. The clothing too is coming apart, the sort of tears in the fabric that make no sound. In this photo the clothing department's team of tailors, sitting on their tabletop, make a new suit of clothing exactly like the old one. The skin, meanwhile, over the dark and stitched, naked man, gets a coat of paint containing a dark preservative, which is re-lightened with a second dye. They find a match for Eric Polle's hair color in a drawer marked "Taupe," and glue the fine strands into the scalp all in one direction, then all in the other. They reapply his cowlick as well. At last they reattach him to his bench and reunite him with his canister of coffee. Workers also take this opportunity to erase signs of vandalism.

This treatment has erased all personality. Eric Polle now greets the visitor with a blank neutrality, an almost beatified, professional and generic willingness. The smile in the catalog picture directs neither inward nor outward but toward the very idea of theory, stripped of theoretical particulars. There have been calls to change Polle's hand back to the original.

Perhaps the hand is in storage somewhere.

Theaters

IT IS TIME TO CLIMB down.

We enter a tunnel to the side of the station. Down we slope into the dark. Emery says we are going under the buildings of the diorama. We come out at the Theater District, a narrow street lighted with parlors at the fronts of teahouses and drinking establishments.

We enter among the crowds. It is mid-evening here. In the street the typical merriment at tables. A man with a violin in the back of the place near the mantel, elbows a-jaunt, plays with a kind of pathetic strain to his expression. Lovers, slightly lascivious in their grins and gestures, lean toward one another, or dance spontaneously. Yet their eyes can't quite meet. Mr. Emery shows me a path through the crowd at close quarters, between the greater body of people and men leaning, smoking cigarettes (which glow but are not lighted) against the shopfronts. One man lights a cigarette for another, each making a shell with his hands. The flame is a little shard of celluloid. They are unshaven and appear resentful. A few other men stand at the mouths of alleys; arms crossed, they wear aprons, suggesting that they work in the kitchens.

Dark comes down suddenly. The theater marquis are all lighted pink and red and green. The people's faces appear as flowers or light-giving moths. We wind through the people in the lobbies, to the inner theaters. Even backstage. The plays are frozen in place, complete with audiences. There are some rather risqué dance routines in the shadier theaters, the dancers positioned in ways you can well imagine. The audiences sit in the dark, and all the stages glow like yellow and gold aquariums. There are waiters with drinks. Behind the curtain, the sound crews are hard at work with bellows and a bevy of odd machines.

On our way out of the last theater, Mr. Emery comes to a sudden stop at a man who stands in the entryway.

"Look," he says, pointing at the man's hand. "You see, sir?"

The hand forms an odd shape: the thumb crossed over the palm. The tip of the thumb touches the ring on the ring finger, as if he were signaling the number four.

"He's putting his ring down with his thumb," Mr. Emery says.

Emery wears a look of joy. But I feel uneasy. I look around, trying to see if the man is signaling something: telling us something having to do with the number four. I try to cluster together things in view. I can't find what is being said, but Mr. Emery is in a state of wonder. About the inevitability of the hand. It is inevitable that you will use your thumb that way, if you wear a ring. We all do, he seems to say.

Clowns and Mimes

THROUGH THE PEEPHOLE THERE ARE six. We see them in the dressing room, the transition cupboard between the lives led in the Town and the performance in theater. We find ourselves in close proximity, as if we ourselves were one of them and must also prepare for the stage in this tight-sanctioned moment of hurry. Mirrors. Yet due to the angle (necessary for the thing to come off), no reflections can we see. And so we are spared the nesting-cups of sight that we have come to expect from works of the era in question. With the Diorama of Clowns we peer into dormancy, into suspended animation.

Yet the clowns are in flux. Some returning from the stage and others, in a frantic state, preparing costume and face. They reach across one another. We see the gestures we have come to expect, as well as two new signs, signs unknown to us before. The eyelines are consistent and therefore not meant to alert the viewer to hidden text.

The details are carefully intended: the open drawers, the cosmetics cases with their lids yawning. The poof has fallen to the floor, a deliberate accident very difficult to achieve in the diorama. The rack of costumes, so very like our own but made absurd. A ventriloquist's dummy, nonplussed in the open carrying case. Each clown of the six crammed into the dressing room is self-bent in the difficulty between performances, nearly called to the stage (the stage manager, you see, leans into the room at the open door with her clipboard).

Who is pressed to vacate the dressing room for the next act? There are beads of sweat (composed of beeswax and lacquer) on two of the heavier clowns, at the forehead and temples. This woman has her wig off, her hair matted to her skull. She is about to return the wig to its wooden ball where other wigs reside, the hair under her arms prominent as she stretches over the great clouds of color.

But in the corner stands a mime. We are meant to see her reflection in the mirror, hers alone, watching them through the naturalism of the very air, an arrangement rather heavy-handed, to be sure, but the mime is alone, her hands form the gesture of the clown in her eyeline, one palm cupped, the other tweezed, as if to hold the little pomping-pillow which the clown uses to powder herself. Her mouth, the mouth of the mime, is open as wide as it can go and perhaps a bit wider, in a scream of some sort, echoed in her eyes.

As for the greater array, a very careful effort has been made to indicate that nothing is happening, and even that nothing will, or can, occur in this little room.

I note that no clown looks into the mirror here. There is no indication of menace. Perhaps the short sleeves of this clown in his undershirt, the wrist hairs, the bulging, the chest hair; otherwise, a placidity floats over the world. There is, as in those dioramas of wildlife, a severed, but partial, narrative.

That the clowns are alive and frozen in time. Others have argued that the clowns—and of course by extension others in other displays—are actually moving, that they have reaccepted the burden of life which had passed from them. An arbitrary timescale is often cited. A single breath, this clown, she takes in five hundred years, or three hundred. This sort of thing. A heart rate of a single beat in a decade. We would appear to them as a river of flesh and faces, peering into the fishes of ourselves in the little peephole, a speedy river flowing through the hallway. Could it be that this is why none of the clowns peers into the mirror, for to see one's own face like that, continuous, would be torture, unable to look away?

A Coin

IT IS WARM IN THE hallway. There stands in one corner a little gumball machine, and I think to lift my spirits with a gumball. Perhaps the sugar, and so on…I ask if the machine is part of the diorama, and Emery says that anything in the hallway this side of the peephole is, technically, out of the diorama. So I obtain a coin and buy a gumball. It is white, like the clown makeup, and I remember once long ago examining my teeth marks in gum, putting it back inside my mouth to chew them into another shape, unable to believe I had made them, not wanting them to remain there. So with my teeth and my tongue, I pulled the gum over itself, like kneading a tiny piece of dough, until the marks were gone.

And I think what Emery has said is patently false. For there is nothing in the Town that can reasonably be said to exist outside the diorama. I wonder how long my coin will stay in the machine and, even as I chew, what to do with the gum when I am finished.

Influence

WE DEPART THE THEATER DISTRICT by way of a "country road" of distant buildings fronted by dry orchards, and soon the train pulls away. I cannot help but notice a change that has come over the Town blipping past, a marked change that you can feel but scarcely name. The character of the displays grows sharper, the details more perfectly executed. The gilt lettering on the pubs. The clean glass. The perfection of the tailoring. The women's hats enormous. When I remark as much to Emery, he nods and explains that from this point forward, Goll had taken an even greater interest in the workmanship of the Town and also that the conservators had recently finished their work. There are many more families than before. They are together, dressed as in portraiture. They stand in windows. They hold hands on fire escapes and on rooftop gardens. As the countryside passes, you see them. They are gazing outward as if at the passage of the train, just as country people used to do. They would stop what they were doing and watch the great beast go heavy by, leaving its layered white and black garment behind.

These people regard us; I feel their eyes. Through them, Goll is marking us. "We mark you in the smooth realm," where life is. "And when you are gone, we'll begin again."

Records

"It takes something inhuman to tell the tale of the inhuman," Smithe used to say. Does it then stand that if a human being appears in a story in any capacity whatsoever, then the tale is human?

Minister Goll enjoyed the notion that whatever you had done or accomplished in the outside world, he could make you into your opposite. In the Town, bankers became janitors. A rival minister became the most flamboyant of beggars, wearing only a suitcoat, his member displayed incredibly small.

That Goll destroyed all official records of the transformation meant that, for him, the pleasure was private. Only he knew—until, that is, such home records as journals and letters began, much later, to flesh out the detail. He liked to stroll the dioramas that were under construction. To give instructions, to change things abruptly if they weren't to his liking. He would dismiss some of his best workers, claiming that they had misheard earlier instructions. There was always the danger that they themselves would end up in the diorama in some humiliating capacity—brushing one's teeth without any clothing on in a little bathroom high in some apartment complex.

"I have a place for them," he would say.

His chief enemies are positioned near the entrance to the Town. And now, those specimens, farther and farther away from the entrance, fade out, yet when I look out again, they are made more real by our motion as the train slides by. A woman seems to be just arrested while washing an entry stair, a little girl while poising on one toe over the hopscotch grid, with its numbers chalked on the pavement. I stand up to get away from the window, hands on the seat backs to the end of the car. But I can get no relief here. Through the window I see into the next car: a porter's white gloves sprout four wine glasses with which he sets the dining tables. He jerks strangely. Stiffly palsied, round fishes sway on the glasses. His hair bristles as if with static electricity where it protrudes from his cap. His face quietly reasonable. He has been this way for years.

Early visitors, before the closure of the exhibit, spoke of a "perfect world." But we dismiss them. They were partisans. They were guests of Goll. They were inside. We are outside.

The train is coming to a stop.

Emery

ON GROUND AGAIN, MR. EMERY checks his watch, startles, and informs me that he has to make a phone call. I try to imagine why.

He leaves me in the middle of the road and steps among the revelers of a town festival which we have stumbled into. Between a hardware store and an empty shop, whose window is covered in newspaper, he opens a hidden cabinet in the exterior of the building. Inside is a red phone, and before he can swipe it away, I see a rotten apple, sagging on the phone top, and a note in block letters: LIL PUF HEAD.

Emery dials, grinding the rotary dial with his finger, and stands for some time, his back to me, his neck gone bright red, talking and listening.

Phone held with his chin, he carefully folds the note and slides it into his coat pocket. Hands free now, he grips the phone. He has tautened against the fabric of his uniform. Near bursting. His conductor's hat is, I now see, too big for a man so short. His head is at the same time small and bony and yet too round on the sides and utterly flat in the back. His shoulders are boylike and slender. There is a pimple on the back of his neck that grows whitish as his neck flushes red. I look away.

In the window of a bicycle shop opposite, a proprietor is showing a little girl a bicycle. She looks up at him. The frozen glass of her barrettes. The man's hands are black and greasy. He is gesturing toward the chrome of the handlebars. When I look back, Emery is making fierce little jerks of his head to punctuate his words. I feel I hear street sounds, but there aren't any.

If Emery isn't careful, I am thinking, he will give himself conniptions or one of the different types of ulcers. He is considered a joke. He knows it. Yet his stiffness of manner—it isn't him. He is young; he is good at his job, I see. Your colleagues never forgive such a thing.

He hangs up the phone.

Emery

RETURNING TO ME, EMERY SEEMS to hold his breath, waiting for me to say something. I let on that I haven't seen the sign. Instead, I make a comment on the cornices of the street. Two stories up, bricks angled and edged out into fascinating alcoves and shapes. Again, that thin smile appears as Emery directs his gaze upward.

He nods.

"The masons keep very busy," he says, his face going through several tortures, each worse than the one previous. He tells me that here and there, after the fact, workers had added signs of weathering—dissolved pointing, rounded corners, streaks bleeding down. They were master masons, he says, "venerable old men," nearing retirement.

"They don't make them like that anymore," he adds, but the sentiment sounds hollow, put there, I feel, for my benefit. But his eyes have gone inside. He is beginning to regain control.

Then I ask Emery how long he'd been working in the Town, realizing my mistake too late. I have implied his inexperience. He knows I know.

He smooths his pocket, keeping the hand in place.

"Three months," he says and lifts his chin.

How does he like it so far? I ask, again putting my foot in my mouth.

He colors. Then, in an act of will astonishing in a person so young, he shifts his entire being, he stands up taller, reassumes his pride.

"There's nowhere I'd rather be, sir."

Two Dioramas

As we walk into a zone of apartment blocks full of shadow, something familiar catches my eye: integrated with the foundation of a building (the mortar lines, too white) is a Michaux diorama that has been taken out of the museum.

Growing out of the foundation is a volunteer apple tree, complete with green fruit shaped like knuckles and covered in worm scars. A cat in the tree, a pregnant female with grey stripes, reaches for a songbird of no known species, green and blue, its head thrown back in song. The cat has almost captured the bird. The whole scene, tree, cat, bird, leaves, appears slightly bleached.

Stooping, I find the edge of the diorama, exposed under the gravel and scrawled on the wood, in a groove, an MDNS number: $G^{186}(0$ —the remaining half concealed in the grit. Only Goll could have authorized such a thing. By their nature dioramas are not moved, except into the protection of storage. But then I remember, isn't the Town a place of storage—of entireties, of wholes?

Now that I have discovered one Michaux diorama, it is not difficult to spot others: diminutive little moments of detail pressed into the dry medium of the landscape, integrated with Goll's project. For instance, in the kitchen of a small wooden house which has been squeezed to shadow between two apartment blocks, a Michaux kitten stands on the back of a dog, whose tongue is out in the mild worry of a creature trying to determine what is expected of it. Dog fur only partially covers the steel rod connected to the kitten's rear paw. Meanwhile, the family stands around a kitchen table littered with newspapers, schoolwork, and glasses half filled with water. Two little girls—twins—and a father, wearing grins that don't quite come off, look at the dog and cat, and in the near hall, just visible from the kitchen, the mother stands on a chair putting something into or taking something out of a metal cake tin, whose lid is partway open. I think it is a roll of bills. Over her shoulder, she tensely watches the family in the kitchen.

Outside the house, I look up. In one of the widows of the apartment building a man about her age watches the house. Lastly, in the nearby playground, a little girl, dressed identically to the twins, bites a boy on the hand. The boy's expression reaches for surprise but doesn't quite get there. The girl's nose is bloody, and through tear tracks, she wears an expression of fierce concentration. Three Michaux sparrows look on.

Under Construction

WE MOUNT AN ELECTRIC BUGGY and ride through narrow streets that open all at once onto a scene of transition, something like a construction site. A vast recreation of shanty towns is being dismantled. There are shipping crates stacked nearby, the kind they assemble with nails. There are no workers around. I ask what is going on, why dismantle the shanty towns, what had Goll meant in putting them there, this sort of thing. "Rats," is the explanation given by Emery. A laugh escapes me. "Real rats?" I say. I don't know myself whether I mean it as a joke, as a way to test the ice, to touch sides.

But Emery only smiles. Are they being relocated or torn down? He says they are to be replaced by parks and neighborhood houses, in order to get the "nuance of life." It seems a made-up phrase. The plan called for a chain of ponds mixed with grasses and trees and for a row of brick buildings meant to front the intervening meadow. The backs of the buildings would be finished too, and the viewer, if there ever were to be a viewer, would approach from the front stairs and look into the rooms where the residents would be going about their lives. The project was in sketches and "just about ready to be modeled." Is there some other message there I have not seen?

I make another joke, this time about the absurdity of moving the poor out of a place like this—I don't recall my exact words.

Emery only presses his lips together, achieving a neutral expression. I think my joke goes over his head.

Indeed, I keep waiting for a moment where something Emery

has said in connection with the scene before us—the construction equipment, the shacks, the trucks, the lifts—will reveal a great contradiction, a great irony, I suppose a kind of gasp in which only I could share, but the moment does not arise. There is no opportunity, only this wide-open place and the sense that we can't see it all and that it has been planned down to the awareness, down to a gesture inclusive of change. At that moment, however, a flash catches my eye: across an exposed skylight, high above even the tallest buildings—some accident of concealment—the passenger pigeons are flowing. We watch them for a moment in silence, moving over what must seem to them long grey buildings, behind the windows of which flicker the buildings of a town, another city under the cover of a building miles and miles long, and on the skylights of which they land. Below them are children in playing postures. Machinery gleams. The trees are in bloom. A frozen train sparks without moving. The tracks thin as hairs.

And that night, when I finally sleep, calmed by the sway of the train, I have a dream of the world before; all creatures surround me and are watching me. They are real and unreal, alive and dead. They are, the dream gives me to understand, placeholders for later times. They are biding their time till they will enter the diorama.

VII: TO KNOW

Harvest

THE PASSENGER PIGEONS ROAR OVER the City. In their billions they come in waves. The dead fall out of the passage itself: birds who meet with accidents against tower sides, the unseen guywires of water tanks, high overhead, old pigeons making their last journey. The dead exfoliate as from a great, grey leviathan. The rising roar of each wave, comprised of single birds weighing sixteen ounces and traveling at sixty miles per hour headlong, begins like hailstones heard a few blocks away and builds to a howl, toward the waiting people.

The city permits each household to harvest two hundred birds. The Fish and Game officers are unclattering their bicycle offices. They fold down their panels and arrange their papers as the droppings fall on their canopies. The birds plummet like rolled-up newspapers to tumble in the squares. The officers verify. They record permit numbers. They weigh the catch.

Meanwhile, households work quickly. At sunset the harvest will be over and the taking of birds prohibited. Boys and girls are bloody up to the elbows on building tops, in the squares, in the parks. A festive atmosphere, interspersed with a grim hurry. The children wear the old shirts of their parents backward, and they are plastered all over with pigeon down, their bare feet having grown plumage. The odor of bird innards blankets the city. The guts are thrown in a pile for feeding to the pigs. The feathers and bones go for meal and compost.

A great deal of blood accumulates in puddles. Cheerful shouts carry over the crowds. Cleavers report on cutting boards on makeshift tables. The red eyes of the birds are half-closed, their heads and necks a confused tumble of wings and feathers.

Over the city the pigeons crash, over the clock tower Opium Ben shivering the air with its bell. Over the harbor and piers, they misshape every surface, softened with themselves, as a mold. They peck offerings left by those who see them as a god. They drape themselves and fall.

The rain begins, and the feathers and skin and the severed feet (some with number bands attached from some distant counting effort) flow out from puddles, the palms of the feet pink, like tiny fingers. All is drawn toward the drains. The undersides of the wings are speckled with green feces. Loops of innards uncoil and, caught, wag in the water and turn white.

The day bends, and the light, too. The clouds clear, but it is still raining for a moment. The sun, as if all at once, is going down. The shadows are confused by their own shapes, long, oblong, and there seems to be a source of illumination behind all objects, on the far side of things, turning the shadows yellow. In the half-dark the pigeons fly, blocking the light. There is a lull. All over the city, they are beginning to roost. Tree branches crack under their weight and awnings sag. The squares grow cooler. From nets, men and women collect the dead that remain. They throw them down from the buildings into deeper nets. The processing continues. That strange smell rises, warm as an untaken bath drawn flat and silent. The people now work with grim expressions and hollow eyes. Salt hisses out of sacks. The washtubs are filled with floating matter with a curious hue, not quite pearl, not quite grey.

Here and there, kittens with their ears cocked have located birds that are not quite dead. They paw experimentally and leap back. In the quiet, sparrows take up the last, twilight machines of their call while raw hands pack the salt. The mechanical pigeons are put aside for repair.

That night, the one-eyed pigeon roosts next to one of them. Its silver breast shows under the feathers, reflecting traffic on the boulevard, and a nearby wire unnerves her. A sensation rises. There are voices creaking in the wire, thousands. Please. Hello please. Language up through the palms of her feet. Billions of words in the cord.

Unnamed

I HAVE SLEPT SURPRISINGLY WELL, aided no doubt by a personal decoction. Daylight finds us rushing in a trough of land, a sort of countryside running as a park through this city. For hours, all during the night, the train has been rolling. It occurs to me that I have missed hours of the Town. And now, still, over this farmland, slung with electrical wires and punctuated by the usual iron bridges and municipal banks, factories for tile, bedding, tchotchke in glass and ceramic and so forth, the train runs. We have picked up speed. I realize furthermore that the Town is built much like our city, and much of the offices and dwellings must be under the ground, like ours. You can see skylights in the middle of pastures and on medians in the small cities, grocers, flower sellers and such—everything you could wish—under the ground, as if to protect against a similar aerial bombardment, and that each one is, as Emery puts it, "enumerated." But above all, faceted, all the people going about their gesture underneath us…and that the building of this place had gone on for years, picked up by other Ministers, in a kind of agreement. As you well know, the project continues to this day.

Hospital

THAT SECOND DAY IS A whirl of stoppages followed by tours of the places in the small city we have come to. Mr. Emery takes me to a hospital where there are wax plants in the lobby and in one of those "connectivities" impossible to make in Geographic Dioramas: story. Down the hall, Emery shows me two birth dioramas in adjoining rooms, one a natural birth, the other a caesarian. One mother is giving birth—the head has just candled—in sweat and strain, the other while sleeping: a yawn of incision, the hands plunged, the nurse waiting with a cloth. Outside the windows the forest begins. A water tower emerges from treetops. In the lobby an old man waits with a young man, their hats maintained between fingertips. One of them, Emery explains, is waiting for *a third person* who turns out to be a woman. She is anesthetized on the table, and the doctors are amputating her leg. In another suite an attendant is wrapping a person in a shroud. In another room on another floor, maggots, like small puppies, clear the dead tissue from a woman's knee. The family stands around. All, including the patient, are laughing at some joke. The daughter, the littlest, has a stuffed elephant with a wind-up key in its back.

Several other surgeries are going on in the surgical ward. Two doctors root around in someone's bowels, some of which have been placed on the chest, out of the way. The face of the person is covered. A third doctor looks through a microscope over by the window. We can't see the water tower from here, but far below at the edge of the lot, several dozen trash bins collect blackbirds as if all at once. Another patient—slide—receives a wrist repair, the arm draped daintily with paper in which a window for the incision is cut. The tendons appear like piano strings. Rolls of black stitching on little bobbins of varying gauges stand on a rolling cart. They look like people's hair rather than silk. Finally, in another room doctors remove part of a man's skull, his brain looking remarkably like intestines.

In the basement morgue a pathologist is cutting up a man. She has taken the skin off his arm and opened the abdomen. An assistant takes notes. A wooden radio stands well away from the table which drains the blood through a hole into the floor. Down the hall the custodian sits on a discarded loveseat drinking from a bottle near the mouth of the orange incinerator. A swept-up pile of medical gauze and paper wrappers awaits the dust pan which has been left leaning against the wall. For some reason the custodian is missing one arm. Perhaps he is meant to be a veteran of some war and earned the job that way.

The depictions of death in particular are quite well done: the slack exhaustion of the mouth of the "dead" person, the repose as the sheet is about to cover the face.

In the kitchens, staff are preparing food: boiled potatoes, mince with onion, pudding. In the administration wing there are even hospital administrators, talking, having professional disputes (if the hand gestures can be believed). I get the sense they are, all of them, there for the woman in surgery, there for her alone. But this is only because she was the first patient we had seen in the hospital, and so naturally, I would draw this conclusion.

All these figures stand in. Like understudies at the theater, eager. The woman never needed the procedure. Her body is being put to use. Her leg is being cut off. Imaginary blood leaks around the calf. Also, according to Goll's method, the doctors are not doctors. There's no telling what they were. But they do everything properly, just as if they had been to medical school at the Farmers College. In the lobby the two men don't even pretend to wait. They have no need to pretend.

This story (their waiting, the association with the patients), which Emery points out to me and which I would not have seen otherwise (he called the younger man, "the husband"): this and every such tie among the figures of the Town *can be made to be suggested.* There is a scar on the throat of one of the doctors, a real flaw in the skin as opposed to one put there afterward, after he had died, that looks suspiciously like a bullet hole patch, or I suppose a tracheostomy of some kind. And there are scars on both wrists of the senior physician, and the liver spots are painted, and his hair—a silver benevolence under the surgical cap—is a wig. They had been prisoners of some kind, I feel. I don't say so. But on our way out, as we enter the elevator, an old man in a wheelchair is smiling at something the patient transporter has said, and the receptionist on the ground floor is on the telephone—and I recall seeing a nurse on a telephone at one of the hallway stations and I think, they are talking to one another, these two. They are saying something just about to be said. Every one of these people has been (I suppose the word is) narrativized. Someone has taken the time.

This happens in the gap in the phone call.

At the back of the hospital is a great boulevard. I forget the name. The cars and the wagons rush without moving. Dust clouds hang somehow in a haze. There are newspapers in the gutter, and dung. Even the pools of urine, speckled with straw, reflect the buildings.

On the median are several apple trees, stepping up the avenue. Mr. Emery approaches, reaches up, and twists an apple off the tree. There is a little click, as of gears. He shows me the attaching piece and then clicks the apple back onto the stem. And then he looks at me, a beatific certainty in his eyes.

The Bay

LATER, THE TRAIN BENDS TOWARD the "coast." The sea is stormy here,
huge slices of resin have been lifted and curled down into culvert
shapes crested in foam. The tide is in. A long sweep gives onto the
blue approaches to a Bay. I see the silver water and the ships, and as
we slip between warehouses down a hillside, the train slows; all is laid
out before us. In this "fishing village" that the city of the diorama has
absorbed, the diorama is dun and colorless, as bland as the black rocks,
covered in barnacles, resting now at low tide. But there is no smell. At
last we come to the slim pleasure ships—they are full-sized ships—
great structures of two and three smokestacks, and Emery shows me
yet another diorama of work.

In the ship's galley the cooks are all bent, the chef among them
leaning into the steam. The dishwasher has just wiped the porthole
with a rag. Note the arch, the streak. A fly has landed there. All of
the kitchen workers have their backs to us. The faces here, strangely
enough, have no eyes or eyebrows. The noses, too, are left off. Only the
portion of the countenance, the potential for a face, that the viewer can
see, has been finished. Here, the face is an oval, collapsed inward, the
stitching as on a ball, pursing lips that seem to have been sewn inward,
or removed. A scab on the back of the elbow of one cook arrests the
eye, but there is no treatment on the front of the arm. The arm hairs
end out of sight of the viewer.

But this skin clearly once belonged to a person, and we see that
he had the habit of the needle. The scars have survived, like islands,

the general process of the taxidermy. After taxidermy, it should be said, a wound doesn't come through but appears as a "flaw." Thus, an injury must be reimagined, then created. This scab was done in one of Hastings' workshops and placed on the elbow with glue. And therefore it is a mishap that never occurred, save in and of itself, as "craftsmanship."

Given that these ships are pleasure craft, the display must have been intended to convey opulence somehow. Yet when we are inside, looking through the peephole of the wall, an inner quality and a curious intimacy takes over. For example, we can see through a porthole another ship, of a bled maroon and white, even the Plimsoll line in gold leaf, and we're struck by the realization that this ship in the distance corresponds to no ship that we have seen in the harbor just a while ago. For this is a model ship, very near the porthole, a quite *little* ship in real terms, done up as the twin of the ship we're in. Portholes bulge with that pertness of all models, that gleam on the false water, and on the other side of the ship are the braces, the naked, tongue depressorwood, the blobs of glue, for this ship, like the galley workers, is finished on one side only and suddenly, that feeling, that twinge of intolerability—a total vertigo—tells us that the twin galley, the twin porthole, the twin meal, and in the wall another porthole wiped of steam, and beyond, the twin galley porthole of another ship rests at anchor. And yet we know full well we've just traversed the docks and have witnessed the fly in the upper portion of the porthole. Until we remember that the fly as well must exist further on, endlessly, lensed with other flies.

Doubt

IT IS AFTERNOON, THE NEXT town approaching and fleeing away. At one point while we rush, the train never sounding its horn, I look up, suddenly remembering the ceiling, and I can just make out that a spring snow has fallen over the roof of the sheds. I see the purple clumps in the skylight as the sun is going down. The diorama, too, grows purple as the train hurries through. I ascertain that we are traveling north, because the city that we have left behind had been well into spring. Yet I can't tell how far we've gone.

Meanwhile, the train stops every now and again to pick up maintenance personnel. They have raw faces and helmets. I imagine them filing into the last car which I can't see once they have passed beyond my window. In these arrestations of movement, the maintenance outposts always stand there in the distance, blended into some cluster of period houses blotting out hills and trees, and each species of tree is positively *made* against the black sky. This must be, I think, a light-taken place.

I gather none of the maintenance people know Mr. Emery. Or perhaps it is they who put the sign in the phone box. There is something about their response to him when he steps down and goes among them.

And then we are sliding along again. Villages pass. Or do they?

This question bothers me greatly. I can't let it go, and I remark as much to Emery. He changes the subject, but his eyes drift, as if he is thinking to himself.

You see, there is no geography to the Town. I suddenly feel convinced of this. None of this is happening. It is an easy matter to give the illusion of travel. To shake a train car. To move lights across the gloom of a window. Roll backdrops into place, great scene walls. This is a false place. The train never moves, only the scene. This sounds absurd, even to me. But in this moment, I can't shake it. I feel naïve. I look around me. The vertigo. I cannot shake this conviction.

Verification

AND DO YOU KNOW WHAT Emery does, Jeffrey? You wouldn't believe it, but his response is his first act of kindness toward me. Night has come on. He steps to the telephone at the end of the car. He speaks into the receiver. He clenches his jaws. He is gesturing with his finger.

Slowly, the train shudders to a stop. By some authority I hadn't realized he possessed, he's phoned the engineer. Outside the windows, dark spreads everywhere. The windows of our car are painted on the ground as yellow rectangles, rippling over sudden grasses and horsetail weeds.

He helps me down into the fields. He holds a barrel flashlight, because for some reason the kliegs cannot be turned on at the moment, and there, in the cone of light, is a farmer on an old-style tractor with steel wheels that are encased in mud. He is cultivating the corn after (it must have been) a soft rain. Raindrops glitter on the leaves.

Corn, about shin-high.

By all evidence, there should be moisture in the air. Loam. Drips from the leaves. All of that. But the field is empty that way. A world without weather. You are left in an absent mist. The farmer's face sends back the light of the train windows, crackling, one lacquered fist on a lever. He wears a wedding band. There is no wind.

The stars painted on the ceiling make bold arrangements in their frost of silence: chaotic stars in the smoke of the heavens. You can feel the space, the size of the great land beyond. There is no mistaking.

I ask what lies beyond the farm. Emery says the River Rye, and at the heights of the other side, a bluff and apartment blocks rising in tiers, "in rows," I think he says. But the lights are off. And ahead, you can hear the rumble of the train sent back by the woods, in bellied heat. I accept at that moment the truth of the Town.

Now, I want to see everything. Its size, its scope. Michaux says, "The most valuable things aren't for the eye, but for the imagination, but in order for the unease to set in—the unease of the imagination—the knowledge that things exist—they must really be there." You feel you put them there; that they are there for you. I feel I am being watched. Yes, I want to see everything. What am I missing, what is withheld?

For a brief moment Emery places his hand on my shoulder.

The Silence of Mr. Emery

AND SO I TRY TO get to know Mr. Emery. Over dinner in the dining car we exchange histories, of a kind. I must confess, his reticence appalls me. He has scrubbed his speech of any regional accent, as far as I can tell. To hide, or fit in. I can't blame him.

Then again, it is also likely my age, sixty years his senior, rather than some trait in himself alone, keeps Emery silent. He believes you speak to old people quietly with a stiff formality. A kind of silence around the dead. I find myself a sudden neurotic in the face of a respect and deference I can't square with the private smile of this young man. But be that as it may, we get to know each other a little.

He is the son of a hospital clerk. His father had left the family early on.

"He made his choice," Emery adds. Yet when I look into his eyes, he seems a kind and melancholy lad.

"Do you have any hobbies?" I ask.

He is a disc thrower. You know the sort. You throw wooden disks to hit posts in a certain number of tries. This game he combines with wood bowling, on the greens in the middle of the woods, and you must strike the post with the disc and then you have gained the privilege to roll the ball on the undulating green, getting as close as possible to the yellow ball without falling into the hole. He tells me all about it. But it is his attendance to the city's Mote Tournament that most arrests me. For Mote is a long game, of the mind primarily, predicated on mystery and a vague unease. It is our national game. A game of old men and newspapers and documents. We chat awhile about the prospects of

Lord Teld in this year's game and whether or not he will be able to assemble a team on such short notice, and with the War going on.

Most of all, I picture Emery in the out-of-doors, with a glow to his cheeks on the course, shouting lustily to his companions, off into the unknown over the ferns. Perhaps he will take a rest, open a box with his lunch in the little compartments and a flask passed 'round against the fall cold.

But more likely, he plays by himself.

Sentiment

I WISH YOU WERE HERE, Jeffrey. That is a fact.
But I won't become sentimental.

Emery

EMERY'S MOTHER HAD EDUCATED HIM—BUT not his sister—at home, he says. At first, I assume this is because the family couldn't pay for schooling, but I am wrong. In fact, Emery's mother didn't approve of what was taught in school, so she kept the boy home, doing her best to educate him, including instruction in manners, bearing, and a strict sense of propriety. She "boxed his ears," he says proudly, and I note the outdated expression. Emery's sister, on the other hand, was a strong-willed girl. With flushed cheeks and a keen stare, she refused her mother's instruction. "She was the smart one," Emery says.

Sarah had made a world for herself in school. She gained friends, won prizes, and at home was even able to help Emery prepare for the more difficult parts of the end-of-school exams in preparation for his entry into the workforce. He credited Sarah with ensuring a high enough score to be accepted into the museum.

Even young—no older than seven—the girl spoke of winning a scholarship to the Farmers College. It was her intention to study botany. She wanted to "make new kinds of trees." To help with expenses while his sister finished school, Emery delivered fruit by bicycle. Then their mother became ill. The disease spread "from her knee." She pretended not to be in pain. He nursed her, gave her morphine. She died at home.

Thereafter, Emery and Sarah lived in several different institutions for children. They were never separated, and their ordeal led to a closeness between them. Then at seventeen, when Sarah was preparing for the Farmers College exam, she became ill, too. The same strange disease. She died six months later.

An Historical Diorama

EMERY SEEMS TO LIKE BATTLEFIELD dioramas because we tour no fewer than three. They are huge battles at different historical moments of our city. Often, Dioramas of History depict a great defeat, a final victory. The largest of these (and his favorite) is the Passing of the Scroll, in which the defeated Smithe, his arm in a sling and standing with a crutch, his footwrap ostentatiously sodden, is just about to sign the Treaty that would bear his name. You know the moment well, from grade school, but I suspect you are unaware that the battle has been redone in the Town. Emery's cheeks become flushed as we gaze over the landscape.

Smoke hangs over the battlefield silence, the flag's lungs sliced through. The two armies fade into the haze. They face off. All is stillness. You can hear the last bird, as after a storm. The armies have put themselves to rights for the ceremony, and it is Smithe's name, rather than the geographical designation of the battle itself and its claim of a hundred *thousand* lives over two weeks, that is attached, like the little graves all lined up whitely, ten to a marker, one on top of the other, to the unfortunate general. The diorama seems to laud him. To celebrate his unwillingness to compromise. Incidentally, to accomplish this feat of burial the graves were dug to a depth of ten feet and the soldiers lain coffinless. For now, however, the dead remain off in the distance, and we walk the border of the woodlots where they had been piled. A chest exposed, the heel of a foot. Arms flung out, bent under, bellies up, some of their members bloated out of shape. Mouths open. One man's wooden dentures partway out of his mouth. We come round to the temporary pavilion of stiff canvas, pale. Smithe stands with the quill, woozy but upright. He will die of exsanguination hours later while dictating farewell letters to his daughter and his wife.

A picket fence, as if dug up and dragged to the side, keeps the viewer away. Distance creates the atmosphere. Through the trees in adjacent fields tiny soldiers in their opposing uniforms stand in ranks.

Next, we travel by train a short ways to the battle itself. This is necessary due to the enormous size. The train trundles past the distant armies. Soldiers relieve themselves along the woods. A tent is being dismantled. Horses pull cannon after cannon. Footprints are pressed into the sands and muds. After an empty quarter, of ponds and swamps bordered by low hills, we arrive at the Battle, and here, the landscape of the Surrender is replicated with an exactness that borders on astonishing. Only now, we are back in time. We have left the train by way of a paved path, the first "museum affordance" so far, with little plaques here and there.

Emery hurries me past the mysterious etchings of brass until we stand upon one of many viewing platforms. Field on field, road on wiggling little road, the troops advancing, stretched over a rolling landscape. "Dust" hangs in the air. We stand above, as if looking through a rustic frame, made of logs cut for some purpose and piled for later use. The ax marks are very lifelike, the beads of sap. There are two telescopes and explanatory matter, designed to appear within the lens, depending on the angle and focus, and the device gives a flaccid little click within, identifying key mythologies as well as verifiable facts pertaining to the battle. You turn this scope with its great head like an old-fashioned camera, and these locations are named The Copse, The Hollow, with a tiny time code pertaining to the short, and devastating, battle clock.

One can also peer with the naked eye. Squinting into the haze and the body of the smoke, it is quite hard to take it all in. But each swivel of the telescope frames another diorama in the great, mauve window, well quiet. The part of the view which is out of focus (while at the same scale) becomes the backdrop. The pink emerges, into layers. Is this smoke? Are these uniforms? Are they the feathers of a ground haze?

Smithe's Fight, of course, gives us, nearest, the left and right flanks of the Battle of Spoon-Etchen (named after the small stream cutting through the fields). Never once did I see the ceiling of the sheds covering the diorama. I looked hard. The sky became a kind of promise, a pink and yellow enormity, the gulls, riding high, a different color than those upon which the rays of the sun had not yet fallen. The depiction here is of the very beginning of the Great Charge. Here is the grapeshot. The men and women swivel the batteries (the barrels point downward as you swing around), which are just about to open fire on the charging soldiers. One imagines that the soldiers know this. The hole of the cannon changes shape in their eyes (but not in our own, for the diorama is inside us all of a sudden, changing shape on its own), from an oval opening to a black circle, and this change is how they know. Secretary Wilder on the far hill (which happens to correspond to our vantage) described the cannon barrels as "thread-sized in the distance, lifting all at once, like black hairs, articulated on an arm by the introduction of a chill." The soldiers keep running, even as they hesitate. They will always be in this posture and in the state of this knowledge. Of all the soldiers I note only one whose steel rod, screwing him into the ground by the heel, was visible.

We cross to the far side of the battle, a trip this time underneath the ground by a little tram, in order to view things from the cannon batteries' perspective. The medical tents of Smithe burst into focus, and the crimson piles, the moist objects thrown outside, the tent flaps limp or tied up in the humid air (we recall it is July in this world), the hurried orders, the shouts, the dispatch runners, one of whom, a girl of about sixteen, extends her arm as though to fall but likely only to pass the leather tube to her superior, a woman with a great, broad chest, large shoulders, who is missing her ear in a blob of scar tissue. There are hash marks on the tent, in black chalk, evidently done in the absence of paper or in the fragility of haste, one can't say. But we don't know what they are counting or how the marks would be washed off, to count again, or whether these marks are always to be there...

To travel the numerous scaffolds of this diorama at their many levels would take several days and would likely yield only boredom. Several times, a viewer follows the pathways under the ground. There are benches in the scooped alcoves where I sit awhile, looking through one of the interior windows, invisible from the vantages above. One or two taxidermied museum-goers stand in silhouette before the windows, so often you can't see properly. Then the next "bump-out," as it is called, beckons one to continue the journey to stop at another alcove.

One can view the diorama at ground level from these bump-outs, also known as pillboxes, where a lump of scenery is heaped up, so as to conceal the viewing window. The soldiers are barefoot. Their black toenails at eye level. Something like cotton candy rests on the ground. Soldiers run in all directions away from a mass of gore, the cannonball, hissing, having struck one of them and failed to explode. The silence hisses and has given the ball a spin in the dirt; the explosive is about to go off. The soldiers flee for their lives.

There is a footprint in a puddle of congealed blood, the dead soldier with his arms flung out nearby. I don't think the footprint quite works, really, owing to the time it takes for blood to coagulate. And also it just strikes one as excessive, even here, in a diorama of battle.

A soldier is seen close. The nostrils loom. The flap of skin. Moth holes at the uniform breast, the collar chewed in the distinctive pattern of the hone moth. A great conservation effort is underway to restore such damage, which is happening all around. Conservators, as a matter of fact, were continuously getting on and off the train when we were traveling over the diorama. Emery explains there is a program at the

Farmers College intended to encourage youth to enter the conservation field, but the conditions of the work, the psychic and spiritual strain, require a certain personality. One can spend months on one area of an enormous soldier, bringing her face back to the slack terror—or is it determination?—in a sea of thousands upon thousands of similar soldiers, shoulder to shoulder. Such an occupation cannot but feel like the task of the world itself, the task of living (where there is always more to do) in a deeply hidden way; a task never finished and which must be retouched as soon as the hand of the conservator finishes its last gesture.

We see anthills clustering the light, like sugar cones, and the ants still collecting things and mounding them up. This little fellow is poised at the top of the cone, his brown body transparent, like a hardened candy sprouting hairs. Here, a different species, a black ant this time, swarms over the dead war pigeon with its purple eyelid. But look at all the waddings, the dropped wrappers. We look through spoked wheels, through pantlegs like a dining room as seen by a child. Birds appear headlong (are they painted or on wires?), their wings swept back. One doubts the wires, for they are difficult to keep clear of lint, the accumulation of which makes them suddenly *domestic* as if the battle, seen from the enclosed darkness of the pillbox, were suddenly a living room, and thousands, if not millions, of such details, strain themselves against one another and yet all come together. No single soldier of the thousands upon thousands and more has failed to receive full treatment. There are, as ever, no half measures. A great effort has been made to individuate them.

I ask Emery why this is his favorite diorama but he shakes his head as if he believes I don't get it. So I ask him again. What is it about this diorama? He tells me, because it is perfect. It is beautiful.

Lonesome

AT DAY'S END, EMERY JOINS me in the compartment. He sits tentatively, as if he were disturbing my privacy. I offer him something, but he refuses. He has put on a clean uniform. The starch almost crackles.

We discuss the death of Minister Goll. How, after the economy collapsed, the crowd, manipulated by his enemies, turned against him, trapped him in the Residence, and after demanding his resignation, burned it to the ground. Goll's doubles couldn't save him.

"It was a mob, plain and simple," Emery says. "They didn't even let him defend himself." I reply that it is difficult to know what there is to defend.

Emery looks at me, then out the window.

To cover the silence I rather unwisely show him the catalogue photograph of Eric Polle, the man on the bench in the lobby of the Town. He gazes into the photo a long time without speaking.

Sitting in the train, we are far removed from the death of Minister Goll. I think of his doubles, created to throw off potential assassins. They were once quite common, and even today, some few mechanical men walk the city. There was a sighting in the papers just the other day.

The figure was like something out of a fairy story. He shambled, a bird's nest in his coat pocket, and three starling chicks poked their heads out every time he stumbled. He trailed copper wire from toes of locust wood. Mechanical men of this vintage often sit for weeks in the same place, absorbing the sun until enough energy has entered into them, and then they move on.

Goll is still celebrated and mourned with "wine and flowers." His strange and bitter, his contemptuous but somehow poignant quip, spoken just before his death, survives in several sentimental songs connected with the anniversary. Goll loved wine and flowers. On the day of remembrance, thick flowers cloud the doorways of places the man frequented. And especially outside the Residence. On the significant days of his mythology, there is always a type of rose, the prairie rose, known now as Goll's Darling, piled everywhere. All living plants were destroyed by an edict of Parliament, but they thrive in private gardens and in the hothouses of Goll partisans everywhere. Goll's Darling, an orange and white oblate cusp, shot through with a heavy lavender, with almost red streaks of threes and fours on each petal.

"Give me the flowers of the men; give me the wine of the women. I shall be fine."

He may have been drunk when he is said to have uttered this little pearl, and whether the inversion was intended, one cannot know—he may have transposed himself at a crucial moment, when negotiations had broken down and the police were laying siege to the Residence. It is difficult to say. Everything about Goll slips. You can only find him in the Town, in other people. His favorite color was said to be green with a little orange running along the surface, like a wood in the light of sunset. He despised books and was said to have loved the idea of "nature" more than the actuality.

I again offer Emery a little something. This time, he hesitates, then accepts. As I mix his drink, we are speaking of Goll's doubles.

"They were made to last," Emery says.

Here are several survivors, rather grim, and bulky, like daft old men who have, by the currency of their isolation, earned a hermitage. Clacking their wooden jaws, all the leather of the face rotted and the latex long in rags, they seem to be overwhelmed in their mental capacities. They plant flowers at the back of an alley. Or they mime such an act in the empty air. They carry objects—a tire from the mud, a dripping pallet—and deposit them in a pile. Every now and then, those that remain appear in new clothing, provided by one Society or another, and they flash fresh at the corner of the eye. The doubles do not always like to be approached. One tailor and his wife were killed when the mechanical Goll, its mind unaware, attacked them while the fitting was in progress. He beat them and tore them and carried their pieces to a pile he had collected in a clearing.

Each double has its separate sort of little cache. They habitually collect things. A cat follows one here. The Goll feeds it. Children throw mud, tie things to the sleeping hulk of a figure, place objects in the open mouth. A cat sits on the shoulder of another mechanical man while he walks, humanizing both of them. These men have become, at times, almost venerable fixtures, Retrospective Automata; they go on without complaining. Here, another double buys coffee with coins stolen from a fountain in one of the Squares; he pours the liquid into himself, reeking of beans that come pouring out intestines of long-cracked rubber, soaking the clothing. He does this again and again. He stands at the kiosk at first light. The door rolls up. Swaying, opening his mouth, the teeth of green-black locust wood are chewing. What does he want?

"He remembers," Emery says.

There must be a life that can be led.

The doubles were built to mimic Goll's eccentricities, his ticks and so forth. And the likeness was astounding. Naturally, they were hunted down at first. When approached, say, in a barn behind the Financial District, they would not fight back. It is supposed they felt no pain when these first individuals (before others were habitually ignored) were burned. The question, "Did Goll really die in the Residence?" comes upon us always. Did he escape and die bald and toothless, a cancer half again his size on the back of his knee? Meanwhile, the doubles still make hand-shapes in imitation of the Minister. Yet the iconography has broken. We no longer have the visual memory of that man at the podium, flinging out his arms, shaking his head with exaggerated disgust.

This double was helping an elderly community, the sort of ten-story building, like our own, one is always seeing with an allotment, a few vines, a few goats and chickens. The Goll helped them move stones to ring round the garden. He carried on through the night and into the next night without rest, till all the stones were moved and stacked. And then he stood for many hours in the same place before turning his head with a jerk and walking away.

"Well," Emery says, standing up, "he's gone now, isn't he."

We speed out of the city. At the outskirts I watch the crowds, positioned so as to be shopping at midday. I am not really paying attention until something catches my eye. One woman in the crowd has moved. I feel sure she had been walking in front of a shop window—where snow sleds are displayed—and has frozen as the train passes by. But a row of buildings obscures her, and she is gone.

Passage

THAT NIGHT, I LOOK OUT the window.

Above, beyond the ceiling and the false moon, I see an enormous eye, regarding me behind the panes of the skylight. The white of the eye, the circle of the iris, the black pupil, a planet of fitted rings, one inside another. A huge forest of eyebrow. This eye, this person, looks down without a thought of any kind. I snatch the curtain closed and lie down again, a cold sweat over me.

When I gain the courage to look again, the eye is still there; only, I have the impression it has fastened on something else, perhaps miles away. I chalk this vision up to something I had taken for pain not long before. But I don't think that's accurate.

VIII: THE SIGIL

The Pigeon

THE ONE-EYED BIRD, HAVING SHIFTED across time, is now a homing pigeon. She is getting used to her new body. She lands on a telephone pole. A dirt track, known as a Legacy Road, stretches out, running between two farms, and the clouds ripple overhead between the skyscrapers. In the hedge the yew berries have begun to fall; pedestrians, flowing past, squash them. The hornbeam hops weigh down, open like lanterns. And on the other side in the Square a girl cries the autumn news. While the fountain splashes, the girl's voice cries out between wagons and trucks, and endless sparrows vanish into the hedge.

On impulse, the pigeon alights on the wire and shuffles herself. She has spent the last year of her new life whirling in circles of a standard shape and memory: to the silo and the barn, past her reflections in the skyscrapers, to the milkhouse, to the secret eaves until she is part of the farm, a part of the map, seen from above. How much simpler this life is. She has known this farm and others nearby. She has known the nearer squares. The workers are repairing the fountain where giant figures who died there gesture outward in dust and shouts. The stone tools ring. The lane is quiet heading toward the corn. A burlap sack falls out of the sky. The goldenrod sags with the weight of flowers, and the lane narrows out of which some shape might be coming. And then, the one-eyed bird is flying again over the woodlot at the edge of which a dog scratches an ear and an old woman contemplates the espalier, yet the bird has never left the wire. The building-channels suddenly open, and close. Somehow, without knowing how, she is flying back again, back to the wire.

This wire leaves her exposed. She turns away from the hedge to check Behind, and the City stretches at the back of the eighty acres, buildings faintly smoky. The fields below, one in sheaves, one struggling toward the third cutting of hay, are cut by a brook, icy warm-brown, its bottom made of dunes, the riffle backing to the plastic water, repeated in the sands, the entire flow contacting the wall and by some mysterious means disappearing into it, into the City. A sensation rises in her. Voices creak in the wire by the thousands, smaller than boys and girls, smaller than insects. Please Hello Please. Who Is Speaking Please. She has felt the flow before through the palms of her feet, billions passing either direction.

The Cart

MIDMORNING (I THINK IT IS the fourth day, I've lost track) finds us trundling along in a sort of old-timey cab pulled in drunken jerks by a mule. We have finally come to the River Rye, that dioramic twin of the river of the same name, which creeps in a culvert underneath. An "Inn-keeper" had packed us a lunch, and the lunchbox with which I have been entrusted jounces and slides this way and that until I finally secure it by its strap to the springs of the seat. We wind our way from the river up into the neighborhoods. Terraces slope down to the left, the stammering roofs stepping off in all directions: irregular, tarred, shingled, with their pretend smoke rising up, then spreading, all in a sheet, above. Mr. Emery is gentle with the mule, the reins slack, and every now and then, he gives a little lift, sending a parabola of leather over her back, followed by a click of his tongue so that she will speed up. The mule flicks her ears and swivels them as if to detach flies. But there are no flies, or they are imaginary to her.

I am enjoying the organic quiet of the conveyance. It has been a while since I've ridden in such a cab. I am thinking these things, and others, when a figure appears in the cobbled road around a corner. We come to a stop.

Standing in the road is a man. He is a taxidermy dummy. A simple workman, making a shape in the air with two hands, as if he played a bassoon that has vanished from his grasp. He wears a leather apron, his cheeks expanded and his mouth pursed. He is a glass-blower, removed from his workshop.

"Why is he in the road?" I say.

Mr. Emery sets the brake and steps down. "I don't know, sir."

He approaches the man and stands with his hands on his hips, looking around as if to locate a vandal. At last, he lifts the man, who maintains his pose with uncanny lightness, and sets him to the side of the road, out of the way. When Emery returns to the cab, he wears a tightened expression. And we go on, faster than before, and Mr. Emery, his jaw set, seems to peer into every corner and behind every wall.

We eat our lunch in silence.

Goll and the Diorama

THE DEEPER ONE'S CONTACT WITH the Town, the greater the conviction that Minister Goll's presence and image are everywhere. Goll appears again and again. His image is mapped onto the hurrying people. Emery would point this out at every opportunity.

Surrounded by children, a corpulent man dispenses candy. He wears a street-sweeper's uniform. He places the handle of his broom against his shoulder, and his free hands fashion ears on either side of his head. He has asked the children something. And now he asks them again, and he expects them to answer in unison. That is the meaning of the ears gesture. The children either jeer or laugh; such is the ambiguity of a human face when under the strain of taxidermy.

But observe the children, please. Note how they all appear the same. Note how they resemble the man as if they were his own.

"Do you see the resemblance, sir?" Emery keeps saying. All of the figures in Man With Candy, call it, bear a striking likeness to the minister. He *infuses* these faces. There is no other word for the coming-forward of our recognition. But we feel we're in error because the dioramic likeness is always a wizening, with a glistening crackle to the cheeks requiring the endless return of the conservator. Even the healthy (the hale street-sweeper, his prodigious belly lonesome for a pint), goes gaunt, and the children go gaunt, as balloons after a party.

Wax would have been the better choice.

But wax is not punishment. Wax is celebration. Wax figures are not visceral in any way; they are too perfect. Everyone appears too freshly bathed. Even the downtrodden are scrubbed to a painful idealism. I suspect, though he wanted perfection, Goll might have been pleased at their decay.

Walking down a little street on a bluff above a city park, one glimpses piles behind the row houses. I cannot prevail upon Mr. Emery to stop. I am convinced (until doubt creeps in) that these are piles of people. I see limbs, outflung arms. We come to a small square surrounded by apartment blocks and maple trees with clumps of monocopter seeds in light green wings. People stand about. A woman on a bench. A man closing his umbrella. An old woman on a balcony watering her flowers with a galvanized can. I am allowed to come close. And here, too, this feeling comes upon me all at once that each and every figure wears some subtle sign of Goll. Not always a likeness, but a *sign*. Note the pinkie ring on the little girl: Goll too wore one of these with his birthstone in red glass, made small for the child. A wrinkle in this old man's coat—as he reaches for the block of ice in the front stoop box— forms a "G" so soft that the mere change of the angle vanishes the very idea that you saw it. The businesses, I have no doubt, bear names significant to Goll. And what of the birthmarks? You will recall Goll had a birthmark on his elbow, a sort of wobbled figure of two circles, one on top of the other, like the number 8, less than an inch long, as if it had been tattooed with the stinger of a bee. This mark I observe distinctly upon the elbows of three specimens in that little square. I find myself, in summer scenes where it is possible to investigate the bare arms, counting these marks. I lose count. Some figures have two, one on each elbow. I see this symbol again and again. What could he have been thinking? What half-madness (was it a sort of grim humor or was it rather sentimentality?) could have pushed Minister Goll—who certainly wasn't mad—to do such a thing?

I believe he felt himself in solidarity with the people he had caused to enter the Town. He saw no keen distinction between himself and others, save that other people stemmed from himself, were caused to exist by virtue of himself. He was "preserving" them as exemplars, and the workshop affixed the birthmarks with glue. In other cases the 8 is painted on. He seems to have a kind of affection for them. Thus, we have before us that singlemost rarity and anachronism: the luxury of the will.

"And what happened to Goll's body after his death?" I ask Emery.

Limits

"HE'S IN THE DIORAMA," EMERY says.

I frown, sitting up straight.. "Really and truly?"

"Make no mistake." Then, as if he feels he'd gone too far, he adds, "Somewhere. Protected. But we don't know where."

"So they can't find him?"

"He's here so as not to be found."

"And hasn't anyone looked?"

"Probably," Emery says in an offhand way, looking away from me.

"But how would we know?" I say, unable to keep the incredulity out of my voice.

Emery looks me dead in the eye. "We know. And besides, he didn't die in that way."

Mythos

EMERY LAYS OUT THE THEORY. He says Goll didn't die that day in the fire at the Residence as the mob gathered round. A double had died, allowing Goll's escape. From an unknown location, the theory went, he supervised the expansion of the Town, which had ostensibly been closed but actually went on as before. He "kept his hand in," Emery says. I assume he means in politics, as well as the Town.

I had heard this before, of course. There were any number of theories, none of them quite plausible, depending on how you saw things. For instance, Goll altered his appearance and hid in plain view as, say, a blacksmith. Among the people. Or he retreated to a bunker, imagined as a place of strength and resolve rather than a place to hide, a place decked out luxuriously or simply, depending on whom you asked. The most absurd theories, and the ones most believed, outfitted him as a shepherd in the hills, or a healer with special powers who walked the tenements, dispensing aid with an outstretched palm among stray cats, dogs under the stairs in the act of birth, all the Michaudian trappings clustering and building the scene. We pass one now, six green birds on a glass feeder, watched by a crow. Whether this is an original Michaux I can't tell. I remark as much and ask Emery what he thinks of that feeling, the feeling of Michaux all around, and he frowns, tipping his head.

He has never heard of Michaux.

Twinship

YET MICHAUX IS EVERYWHERE: IN animals and in people. The little details, especially, marked out how Goll must have instructed his dioramists. He said he had wanted "life, life, life":

The gray jay on the open windowsill, being fed by a farm woman whose table is in the disarray of a recent bread-kneading operation: flour on her hands, under her nails, a canning jar filled to the rim with wine, wine rings in the flour, an expansive smile on her face, her eyes moist. The jay, head tipped, eyes the broken hazelnuts in the spoon the woman holds out.

The back of the cottage has, unusually, been cut away to reveal three generations going about their day in different rooms: grandpa bathing pink armpits, a young man building a model of an antique military vehicle, a young woman standing on her bed, singing, her closet open, hung with homespun dresses.

Outside, a Michaux: a huge flock of starlings is frozen in the air over a fencerow in the act of changing direction. At a certain angle, their warp takes shape.

Residents

EMERY IS NOT ALONE IN his theory of Goll. I'd read several months ago of a group arrested in the vicinity of the sheds. They had brought supplies for a week and were trying to force one of the doors and enter the Town across from a brewery. In rucksacks they carried homemade maps. They claimed—freely and without any sense that they had trespassed—that they were going to find Goll, whose presence had been reported in the midlands of the Town. They said Goll was living in a hut near a flock of sheep that never moved. I picture this Goll, whom (if what they said were true) would be over one hundred thirty years old. An old man, surprisingly fresh. Wearing suit pants that he has patched many times, a look of calm on his face. He's lost weight, he is tanned. He is fiddling with something in a pasture, a pipe for irrigation, or a piece of machinery. To free up his hands he places a wrench on the back of a sheep, sinking it into the wool.

Dermurgy

GOLL SEEMS TO HAVE FOUND certain postures and actions funny. Cannibalism, for one. He may have wished to depict people devouring other people in order to make some claim about what it is to be human. To consume. To eat.

Acts of urination also abound, usually by old men against buildings, or at the edges of urban fields and parks, as this man shows, with his hindquarters clenched in the thrusting posture of great concentration, watching his own activity with a downward gaze. Or this young woman squatting behind a theater.

Groups of children, too, in postures of innocence and brutality, their mouths open, many in school uniforms as if school has always just let out. They crowd around this boy, beating him. There are children everywhere one looks.

These tableaux are everywhere. There is not a feature of this place that hasn't gotten into Goll, and he into it. They are all his things, all his people. Even the chewing gum on the pavements has been put through a deliberate pattern, giving it the birthmark shape. How close must he have held all the decisions. "A sly dermancy," Retherford called it.

Yet: at other times Goll turned the dioramists loose with general instructions by way of verisimilitude. I think even he knew there were limits to what could be done in the Town.

The Boardwalk

We come to a little alley, and down we go over cobbles. We turn in at a door about halfway to the end. In a darkened room Mr. Emery instructs me to look through a peephole in the far wall. Leaning in, I discover another Diorama of Perspective.

We are inside the Vending Machine. We look out at the night city. Three toads catch insects in the light cast by the machine, while across the expanse beyond, a station of yet another fountain pours its dilemma into the sky. Inside the vending machine there are moths, but dead. Yes, we are inside one of the "fine" vending machines of the sort of smooth designing one would wish to see everywhere. There is presumably an awning, though through the double glass—which, with its little fingerprints, light as webs and the gills of little fish, separates the vending machine from the final world beyond—it's hard to tell. All is rose over the sea, the white risers of the safety posts watching the last breakers and swimmers, their dark skin turned blue again.

We are deep at the back of the machine, whose scale is a little larger than it would normally be. The vending screws coil around us. They have a graceful way about their torture, and only a few items line their hoops: a pair of swimming goggles in their box, zinc for the nose in a tube in the upper left, a stuffed bear with a zipper in the back of its head. It too looks outward as we gaze over its tiny shoulder. Emery explains this diorama is one of the few that used to change. Someone would fill up the screws and remove items as well. The screws were often somewhat full, of different items than before. Horoscopes on immensely little screws, in little tubes of paper, all lean one way, like cigarettes. It is said there's a clock within—on a timer, you know—and sometimes the clock…but I am unable to verify this due to restrictions of access. Emery says that often the light has gone completely, as if there has been a blackout on the beach.

The sea is a black mystery; one hardly knows it is there. Only the mauve sands, picking up light from an unknown source, give feeling to the expanse. Are there habitations "behind" us, washing the night? And of course the vending machine itself sends out light to the sands. The bear's ears show larger on the boardwalk, stretched as if a black taffy were elongating. The sweet peanuts fall too, a simulacrum on the walkway, and in the gaps of these shadows there are, as we say, the three toads. Insects on faint wires crowd the beacon. They "fly" in the usual chaos, drunk upon the glass. And the toads hop to gobble them up. That, presumably, is the essence here. No gnash of the soft night. So that one can wish again.

A ship's light we can just barely see through the foam-like skin on the inside of the glass. We make out the back of the machine reflected there. Vending screws disappear into the backing, which of course could not possibly be, because it is we who should appear there, or at the very least some sign of the peephole. There is no back of the machine whatsoever.

Company

BUT AS WE STAND AT the Diorama of the Vending Machine, a suspicion grows. Yes, creeps up on us and grows. I feel someone leaning over my shoulder. Someone observing the boardwalk entire, watching the sun that has dropped below scallops and white culverts of water that almost crash: waves so insouciant they lift their refusal to the beach. I feel It in the scene…It is growing into me. An entity. I can feel his bristles.

I wheel around, and no one is there. To my great embarrassment, I have imagined the odor of the wool coat, but when I turned, the double feeling of that earlier presence was my *new back*. And all at once, he is there again, he is smiling, he is seeing what I will do, now that I have called attention to myself. I feel sure it is him. Surely, it can't be Michaux.

"Are you all right, sir?"

Quiet

THE MUSEUM EXHAUSTION HAS SETTLED on my spirit. For the moment I can't go on. There is nothing for it but to rest. Mr. Emery helps me out of the little alley to a bench at the edge of one of those city parks, paved in tiles, with a monument at the center. While Emery goes off for a cup of water, I take a decoction which I have brought along for just such a moment as this.

I observe the great crowd of people scattered over the park. Couples and groups. All motionless. They are meant to be chatting with one another, but as always the eyelines are off. Each person seems to be carrying on their own, private reverie over the shoulder of their companion, as if everyone has touched on the same thought and were keeping it private, and as if they were looking out for the arrival of a third person in a cosmic infidelity. And physically speaking, something is different about them. They have a strange quality to their skin that I had not noticed before. Woozily, I stand up with the intention of going closer, yet I hesitate. If I am caught in the exhibit, the tour will end. I will be returned to the city in (I imagine) difficult circumstances. I could lose my apartment. I could lose other things. At the same time, I feel I must see.

I step into the crowd.

I approach a woman and her husband. I lean into their faces, and am astonished.

This is not taxidermy. This is embalming.

Taxidermy is general. People become general, everything removed but the skin. Embalming is a specific plea to what remains of the soul.

There is no wooden mold under the skin of these specimens. The understructure is their own. It is clearly made of bone. All of the organs, I suspect (but cannot verify) are inside, stilled and liquid. This clearly is some new method of preservation. And indeed, the signs of the trocar are in evidence on the necks of the two. The man has an odd shape to him, as if he has been broken. Looking around me, I move his sleeve up to discover an additional trocar-insertion point in the crook of his arm. I guess he was the victim of some traumatic accident in which the veins or arteries had been severed, preventing the preservative fluid from reaching the arm and hand, thereby necessitating the extra incision-point. That's what is going on with this little husband in his brown suit, who carries a box under his arm with a pink bow. The blank expression is somehow pliant. There are globules and beads of sweat affixed to his temples and to the upper lip of his wife. They must have been held in a positioning jig, all of them, until their postures "took" and they were infused with the strange-smelling tincture, an odor that hangs heavily, like flowers and certain adhesives, like casseroles made with yams, over the plaza. I try to take this in. The figures appear to be slowly drying. That would account for the sucked-in, wizened appearance of the forehead bones and the wrists, from which the hairs stand up.

I had once read of this process in a white paper proposing the use of some percentage of insecticide in the embalming fluid to discourage molestation of the skin by moths, ants, and mites of all kinds. The author rejected the practice on the basis of just such desiccation as was in evidence here. That paper was years ago. Never would I have expected to see the thing done.

I make my way back to the bench. I am beginning to feel a bit better and thinking of this rare display error—the eyelines and the embalming—and listening to the light fall of rain hundreds of feet overhead (in a far-off humidity) when the air itself brightens around me and prickles. And a vast well opens in the particles of light. In each, a deep hollow of black, soft as black cotton, opens, reaching back and back into an ever-unfolding place. There is some presence there, a great mouth with adjacencies of tubes and throats behind, and this sensation passes, replaced by an undeniable sense of a sea of air that has never been breathed before, coral wastes of a fascinating grey within, like the aquamarine lichen associated with the yellow locust, building in three dimensions, like the innards of a cash register, all done in nickel with shining handles and affordances all tangled, digesting some impossible number, digesting itself in the coral. I can only blink until the feeling goes away, and in that moment, out of the corner of my eye, I catch movement: brown flecking, rustling like paper. Sparrows, bursting into flight, disappear through the legs of the figures with a dry sound. In the next instant I doubt myself. I don't recall hearing wings, even as I hear them, and any chirps maybe the squeak of an exhaust fan. Yet I feel them, keeping track of me from the bushes as if they can't bear to leave.

I stagger back to my bench.

At length Mr. Emery returns with water and a damp towel. He looks concerned. He sits next to me and wets the towel from time to time, and as I revive we look out at the square.

With a rather shy, yet proprietary, sweep of the arm, he says, "I really wanted you to see this, sir. I wanted to give you the time. It is a case of Progress. Real Progress."

He means that the embalming is an improvement over the more primitive taxidermy.

"These are people, sir. They are real, living people. They are here for themselves."

He is looking into my eyes and then outward, then back into my eyes, to verify that I understand.

I nod.

**

Afterward, I feel quite refreshed. In spite of things. Emery really is a kind young man. When he had handed me the towel, damp with water from some hidden tap, I saw that he had written a number on the palm of his hand, in blue ink, like a schoolboy. To remind himself of something.

I don't tell him about the sparrows.

Mother

IT WAS MY MOTHER WHO first took me to see a diorama, and it must
have been in an obscure part of the afternoon when the museum was
empty, because we were alone. I believe she did this more for herself
than for me, and I would wander away, crisscrossing the halls, pausing
only amidst the more magnificent dioramas. And when that failed to
interest me, I badgered my mother for a coin which I would deploy
in one of the many gumball machines positioned near the stairs.
I remember taking note of her as she stood in front of a display—
monkeys in deep trees—a motionless person whom for the first time I
felt was separate in some way from myself. For the first time I caught
something of an internal leaning-in. There was something here in the
museum that she desired. I could feel it. And so I watched her standing
there in her dress and her white gloves and her hat pinned at a jaunty
angle with a little veil attached, speckled in imitation pearls. I could
not idealize her: she was far too volatile for that. Nevertheless, this
mysterious person, watching the creatures whom had in turn become
motionless just for her, I observed for some time. She was there for
herself alone, I felt with a kind of awe. The diorama (and other things,
I was later to learn) had gotten inside her, and in some way, she had
stepped into it.

That day, I had vacillated in front of the machines, tortured between
the purchase of a gumball and a small souvenir encased in a resin
bubble. I had chosen the animal, and I was playing with my creature
along the railings and display moldings. It was a dinosaur made of

rubber, the type of toy, quite disposable, that the museum itself infused with life. You always found yourself at one time or another putting it experimentally into your mouth.

Had she known about Michaux? I don't think so. She was there for her own purposes.

Sheets

As THE TRAIN RUNS, CLOUDS pass beyond the skylight in stately assemblages. I do not see any more birds pass, but once, the body of an airship appears as a long, slow swell of olive and is gone in all of its quilting. My heart seeks out these rare views of the sky. We are now traveling upriver.

Out the windows glimpses of the River Rye, flashing in the light between trees and buildings. As I say, the river itself had been placed in a culvert under the diorama and all the trees had been removed and replaced with trees of painted concrete with silk foliage, artificial moss and lichen. This river drains the whole valley but does not move. And the lift and fall of the eminent trees, stilled here, as if for the first time, is like a dream of a green fireplace in the mind. And just as I am contemplating this, the train slows and stops abruptly. A great quiet comes down. The train then begins to reverse itself, going only a short ways backward, then stopping again. Mr. Emery hurries through the car, followed by several other maintenance personnel. I am instructed to remain in my seat. Emery seems flustered.. As he hurries past, I ask him what is happening. Again, he repeats that I am to stay in my seat, please. And then he commits an error, an error of information. I suspect it is because he's agitated.

He says that we have struck something on the tracks. And then he strides forward, into the next car. I see distinctly that he, and the others, each wear a sidearm.

I go to the window on the other side of the car but can't see forward. I can only speculate. And when the train resumes a half hour later, I see three or four shapes to the side, below a tangle of plum trees, covered in white sheets. Three men stand around, writing in notebooks and measuring with tapes. And though I strain, I can see nothing else.

That night, I am given a boxed meal of beef and lettuces in a soft roll made from wheat and mayonnaise along with a pie of liver and rice and a small bottle of white wine with its own little cork. But I don't feel like eating. Because I am not sure, as I sit in my cabin, if the men standing around the sheeted objects had moved. The train itself had been moving, and the persistence of their attitudes didn't seem quite human in the normal sense.

I seek explanations for myself. I can well believe that if indeed someone had met their end on the train tracks, then they had come to the Town in order to explore. A lark. A dare of some kind. Perhaps adolescents (we had seen such death pacts in the museum proper on more than one occasion, and you would find them in the morning in a diorama, having killed themselves together) had become enamored of death, and they wanted to make an end of it together. Or perhaps, intoxicated, they had just been caught unawares by the approach of the train.

The next day, I again invite Mr. Emery to join me in a drink, and we agree on late afternoon. This is to become a sort of routine for us at the end of a day's touring, I hope. I have brought along a small portmanteau that, when opened, suffices as a thorough little bar. It is my habit to mix a personal concoction when I feel the need, and the habit serves me well, especially in the evening. This expedient had also seen me through the first few days' adjustment to the atmosphere of the Town, when I was disoriented and missing home.

Mr. Emery joins me at the appointed time. He appears at my door upright, scrubbed and in the same uniform jacket, but with, I think, a new shirt, and, pinkly shaven, he looks younger somehow. His sidearm is no longer in evidence. We chat for some time about this and that, and Mr. Emery begins to loosen up some. At one point he says a strange thing that causes me many hours of unease. He says that the Town is "a hope, a real sort of hope." What does he mean? I don't feel I can ask him.

At that moment it dawns on me that he has been too long coming and going through the Town and that he has lost perspective. But then for the first time another train passes going in the opposite direction. The windows are full of light and life; they are the crew, Mr. Emery says, of set decorators, the taxidermists, the builders, the mess crew, the janitors, bound back toward the City Station. They seem, like all groups at a distance, to be engaged in some enviable and lovely revelry. The arm gestures, the reaching for drink, and these little organelles in little squares of light, streaking past, disappear with an impossible quickness. And when the last car passes, a flatbed covered by a mysterious tarp, the River Rye is once again revealed, black and flat, with grey V's of rapids and factories. What had been under that tarp, so large and so angular? Was it a piece of scenery? Was it a machine of some sort?

But what isn't a piece of scenery here?

Though I try, I cannot prevail upon Emery to discuss those earlier shapes covered in sheets.

The Medium

GOLL IS SAID TO HAVE played the lottery, that roulette of the poor, because his mother had always done so. He is said to have won the largest pot ever known and to have continued playing ever after, always the same numbers. These numbers were significant to him, symbolic, and according to the mythology, he won the lottery a second time, though this is obviously absurd. But be that as it may, the funds, according to claims, went into the Diorama of the Town and were instantly devoured by new annexes. As you know it was public money, filtered through the mythology, that built most of the Town. Goll only claimed to fund it himself. How he squared the lottery winnings with hard work, I am not sure, but it likely had something to do with the savvy necessary to ensure his wealth kept growing. Business relationships, careful investing, this sort of thing. And doubtless there is some small truth to this. In a time of extreme economic growth, lax oversight and a public that adored him, the diorama paralleled the building boom elsewhere.

When Goll first decided to put people in the diorama, I do not know.

Memorials

I WALK WITH EMERY UNDER the awnings. A newspaper machine hems us in, a traffic pole and a kiosk. The buses are like superb land ferries, the blue of faces, as for a brief moment, all holding their breath within. The little boys in the street, out of school in their fussy jackets, jostle up to purchase a candy before the journey home. And the little girls, in their socks and skirts, share among themselves a sweetbread. The steam rises as a living creature in the mouth. The light darkens on the interior of hollows (as the rheostat automatically turns them down to simulate a cloud), and the birds peck around shoes. But never mind this. All things are tending toward home, toward events that have already happened, toward comforts, the first fires lighted, the first papers folding into the flower. Toward yesterday the city is growing, inbound-running where the life is secret.

The tableaux in this particular street strikes me because I had seen them so many times. But with this one difference: the names of the children and of the sweetbun vendor and of all the other, secondary actors within the diorama appear for the first time on an etching. Their forms, also, are etched in silhouettes on the brass plate, their numbers within the silhouette corresponding to a list below, revealing the name. They remind us of someone. The names are small, dainty, like the wrists of the children.

"This, sir, is the beginning," Emery says. "The new way."

The historical moment when people chose of their own accord to be in the diorama is well enough documented to require no additional going into here. These children died in an accident when the Q Bridge collapsed onto the roadway as they were walking home from school. The vendor died of a heart attack. In life, he was no vendor but rather an industrialist. His many companies manufactured repeating rifles, buckles, buttons, canteens and the like for the military. Still, the industrialist wished to be depicted as a lover of the people, especially children, whom he loved because they were blameless. Note, he dispenses a sticky bun free of charge in its paper wrapper, his hand gesture refusing the girl's coin. This largess, in that universal gesture of luxury and refusal, the flat palm, marks him as a figure of benignity. Even the coin, Mr. Emery informed me, has been selected for its significance, dull, yet gleaming, the man's birth year stamped upon its surface. The man wears a paper hat.

These dioramas are memorials. They celebrate the taken and are funded by the wealthy, often in concert with organizations of common people. Some of the relatives of the children have paid to appear in the street, and they stand in the distance, in positions commensurate with their place in the bidding process. Goll would have been horrified.

The Vendor diorama employs a rare tactic. There are several layers in an extended depth of field. Those in the back are at reduced scale relative to the figures in front. Their skins, sewn over the molds, a portion of their hair—only what is needed for their representation as little people—make them strangely pinched, like the dolls made from dried apples. It takes a great deal of money to achieve the sort of taxidermy we've come to expect. In scenes like this there can often be two, or three, perspectives in play, with the far plane tilted ever so slightly in order to further achieve visual depth. Thus, the street is a visual trick, partially collapsed in space. Those in the distance on closer inspection are turned toward us for the most part. They watch across the street, to where we stand. Even those in the windows above the awnings, which are streaked with sunlight, the shop names bleached by sun wash, seem startled in the anticipation of an event.

Yet there is the unmistakable sense that something is about to happen above us. Note that the clouds pour inward. Note the old man grasping, but not opening, his umbrella. A woman has dropped her dog leash on the sidewalk. The little dog seems to be wheeling round. One can sense the atmosphere, one can feel the potential of the thing that has begun above us. These scenes are familiar in journalistic photography. They are taken "just before." This is what the people looked like just before their experience of the known would end. It is as if some sound has concussed the street. The people hear it forever. A critic might well point out the slyness and the outright lowness of the placement of such a hidden message in a memorial of the dead. But everyone is dead, everywhere.

Sleep

THE ELEVATOR OPENS ON A long hall, going to the left and right, with windows at each end. Apartment doors go on and on. Mr. Emery opens the apartments without knocking, of course, but the omission of this gesture, of this permission, strikes me.

It is night in the bedroom of this little apartment, and two forms can be seen sleeping, as lumps or cocoons, in the bed. Two, side by side. The legs are bent into the stomach. The sleeping cap of the nearer person emerges from the quilt, a male.

It must be winter.

The kitchen stove touches the bed it's so close. A blue pilot light glows to the ceiling, showing all the metal objects. On shelves. On the range, and the walls. I nearly leave this scene, I can't understand the point. But Mr. Emery stays me. "You see, sir?" he says. "Do you see them?"

And then I do. There are cockroaches. Thousands. Over the range, over the shelves and floor. They cast shadows thin as the light itself.

Emery is delighted at the detail, and I can't blame him. In this apartment building of four hundred flats, each little room is done this way (and we visit at least ten others), all through the night, in darkness and by lamplight, and no one is seeing them. A simulation of life so true to life that it is almost beautiful. That is what Emery is thinking.

And yet even as I look up at that scene, overrun by flies and motes, I realize my experience of Michaux is a nostalgia for a certain lack of awareness. I am nostalgic for a lack of guilt, it seems to me.

IX: THE GIFT

The Pigeon

A BURST OF GREY SUDDENNESS, and when all the birds are gone, a single breast feather, a single piece of down, dry-circles toward the square. The homing pigeons circle round again. The pigeon with one eye rides the top of the flock's plume as it expands like a bomb. The little man far below with the sack of bread crumbs turns his glasses skyward like two flame holes, and her companions' eyeballs are planets cast orange, blazing and inscrutable, even to her.

Beside the one-eyed pigeon (first on one side, then on the other) stroke the homing pigeons. Then they wink out. Gone. Then they reappear as whisperers, too close. In the crooks of their wings, identical birds, like figurines shelter underneath. She shies into the scraps of the wings, dives and rolls against shocks, husks. Through the other side of the flock, cavitating a tunnel of birds, she strafes the top of a hedge. Shaven twigs, clipped needles. Sparrows are dusting in bird-sized holes under hedge boughs, and for the moment she is gone, too, a streak, but she is the catalyst, and before she knows it, the flock has seen fit to dive as if they're poured out of a jar, and the roar commences behind her over the top of the yews, nearer. Now the flock catches her as if her own species were a form of predation, made collective and innocent. She is engulfed. The doubled and trebled birds reappear, their eyes pointed at her as they fly forward with some part of their mind. For the first time they are unfamiliar. As if they have come from somewhere else. As a vague sterling, far underneath, the silver pipes of their wing shafts gleam, but always those eyes: ornaments of sight rather than something that can be known.

Committee

SINCE THAT EARLY TIME WHEN people purchased memorial spaces in the Town, a reversal has occurred. The Committee for the Propagation of the Museum now administers the Diorama of the Town and maintains rights of first refusal over new entrants. If the individual in question has been a criminal of a certain type or has disgraced themselves in some way, their entrance is prevented, and their estate must petition for burial or go the route of the composting plot or to the cremation engines. If, they argue, the diorama is conceived as the ideal of human life and if Goll's excess was a travesty, preserved as a dark caution, what remains is a kinder future with not whims but rules. If an entrant is found later to have committed a foul in violation of the code of conduct and severe enough for censure, their exhibit is removed from the Town and either transported to storage, remanded to the family or placed in a separate wing of the museum (Building Six, Fourth Level) as a separate exhibit, detailing its removal and the history of the reasons why. Meanwhile, the empty space in the exhibit is put up for reoccupancy either completely stripped or in integrated fashion, requiring only another applicant.

Recently, it has been determined that there must be a firm line of demarcation between the earlier times of Goll and our own time, between the monstrous and the new. The question is, how to create such a boundary in such a way that one can tell the difference. I don't think there is a convenient way around the problem if we are to maintain our ethics and continue the diorama *as a place of illusion.* To do otherwise would be to treat the diorama as we treat the world. The medium deserves better.

Indeed, critics point to the very milieu of illusion to say that, after all, what does it matter who is or is not in the Town? Since taxidermy is most often a disguise. The reply is that patrons always have a way of *knowing* history and of celebrating that which is best left behind. The obvious objection comes readily to mind: people will simply bypass the "cleansed" Town in order to contemplate figures, in Building Six, that have been removed. Isn't the ready positioning of all such people in a single place playing into the hands of such instincts? Wouldn't it be better to allow the natural process of infilling (placing more taxidermical figures in the Town) to subsume what is already there? On the other hand, we can't begin to imagine the ideas which are to come. That which has been hidden will always be found.

Economics

THIS EVENTUALITY—DESIRED ENTRY—IS PART OF the economics of the Town, necessary to pay for its upkeep and for its very existence. A curious economy it is. The potential scenemaking near the entrance to the Town and Station White, its chief transport hub, is less expensive than far-flung regions, due to the cost of getting there. But these near sites have filled up quickly and have therefore become more dear. In contrast, a person can purchase an entire fantasy, albeit at great distance from the hub, and outfit it within reason exactly as they like, for of course the scene must fit with the surround. As a result, potential sites, both near and far, are prohibitively expensive. At the same time it appears there is no clear way to locate prestige. Near, with the greater chance of being among other dioramas of prestige but confined in space, or far, with the added largesse, which is made of the pure freedom that comes with size. It is fair to say that prestige is, therefore, everywhere and the inclusion of oneself and loved ones prohibitive in the extreme, except for the wealthy. There are a very few grants made available to the disadvantaged, provided that their proposals for inclusion in the diorama are especially unique or striking in some way. There are also a few sites set aside for the disabled, but these two, taken together, form a fraction of the whole.

Love

THE PROBLEM OF VISITATION PLAGUES US. How to visit the site? In most cases you can't. You remand yourself or your spouse, your family member (and so forth) (and even in some cases, your pet) to the museum, and this transaction explicitly excludes rights of visitation. Instead, a photograph is provided, very fetchingly done, to give proof of location, as well as some solace. I direct your attention to Welk's *Photographs of Dioramas* and specifically to its section on the Town, should you care to explore the subject further.

Knowing you are part of the project of the Town and knowing, now that new laws prohibiting most removals are in place, your loved one's remains will not be disturbed but will exist in a world purely made and in harmony with surrounding things, is a very powerful balm. And there is always the chance you will be selected as one of the ten annual visitors, but from hundreds of thousands of applicants the odds are not chipper, to say the least. This atmosphere of rarefication is a chief selling point. Knowing they are there. Knowing you will be there. That oneself is forbidden, even to oneself, who might wish to look in the aftermath, as a kind of forethought ghost: like an experience of some near-extinct species, known to reside in a region from which we are barred. We don't wish to see this creature. Only to know, and to hope, it still exists there.

Mr. Emery

I ASK EMERY IF HE himself would wish to end his days inside the diorama. His answer surprises me.

"Oh, absolutely, sir."

"But for heaven's sake, why?"

As if struck, he leans back slightly in his chair. Then he recomposes himself. "To be part of history, sir. To be remembered."

Even if there were no records and his name were severed and no one could find him and claim him?

"Oh, there are records, sir," he says in the tone of someone instructing the naïve.

I am stunned, and I can't speak. I sip my drink. I gulp, if I'm honest. I had been given to understand all the records had been destroyed as part of the plan to exonerate Goll, and I cannot square the two stories. But then I remember that in the economy of the new taxidermies, of course there must be records, beginning now. But this is not what Emery means.

"The records are the people," he says. And then, leaning forward with an earnest expression, he asks me, don't I, too, wish to be in the Town? Surely, everyone would choose to, if they could?

I tell him I would prefer not to and that a bit of composting or a simple cremation would suffice. Mr. Emery blinks.. He leans back again, incredulous. He closes his mouth. He has assumed, all along, that I am here on some sort of tour in search of a site, as people used to search for an old-fashioned burial plot. I have one of those moments where I see how others see me, given my age. On the edge of death. I very nearly burst out laughing, not in contempt of Emery but at the simple misunderstanding.

"And are you, yourself, then, planning on the Town?" I say.

At my question his entire demeanor, opened by our daily chats, closes. His entire body is stiff again. An inert privacy closes his face, sealing it from me. Once again, he is holding something back, and though I wish to know more, I can't blame him. He is, I gather, sworn to some professional secrecy. I think of that rushing train, full of staff members in all their capacities, and I can't help but wonder if they have some hand in the recordkeeping, too.

Weather

THE TRAIN SUMMITS A SMALL rise, and one can see for miles the mix of city and country and a huge storm front looming overhead. The storm has folded its body as a seam. I catch sight of the Rye, whose waters have swelled like beer glass around little models of buildings. Even low spots in fields and parks are brown pools. The waters have crept, green and black, up to the second stories of the apartments.

Mr. Emery guides me, once the train has stopped, toward this Diorama of Weather. As we approach the river, by way of a little road strewn with wreckage, small talk is difficult. I am continually stepping over some object or other. Housewares. Torn curtains and their rods. Toys. And then at last, we stand at a low wall.

The vantage is interesting. As if we are submerged, our chins resting on the water surface, we gaze across the flat river to the other side.

Across the River Rye children lean from windows that have no glass. Old men and women in a Retirement Block hesitate at the thresholds of balconies. All watch what passes in the water. They have an angle that we do not, because, for us, the water is only a polished stone floor the color of a beaver pond or a frozen cola. Our mind tries to make meaning of these flattened shapes, distorted by the surface, that are at once laundrian, of the familiar, and shapeless.

We stroll the walkway along the river. A board with nails is level with our eye. Perhaps twenty meters on from our original stopping place, the body of an entire tree trembles, roots and all, in the act of rolling over; it has turned sideways in the river, rootball and branch, and evidently, the submerged branches have caught on some obstacle on the river bottom. And the limbs are lifting out of the water and about to roll upward toward the sky, dropping jewels of blonde water and to crash down in the churn of their green wheel. All the leaves remain. Pristine leaves. Mr. Emery hands me a pair of binoculars and tells me to look closer. Ants cover the limbs and are about to go under.

We move on. As we walk toward the darkened sky, the massive funnel of the tornado comes into view behind the buildings. I can see but an arc—a piece of its curvature—of a much more enormous funnel. Like a spindle bobbin in a factory for upholstery, bulked with terrible accidents, its great passage is not yet complete. The event of its touching down, over there and not here, is still occurring. Debris somehow clouds the sky. The full-sized roof of a barn. A horse and carriage. A wooden water tower coming to pieces, all presumably hung from the ceiling with cables. There is a dusty quality to the air. Green and purple air. The summer is unforgiving and the event is now. I hear an exhaust vent rattling shyly somewhere. And on the far side of the tornado a man stands on a ladder of impossible length. He's bolting something to the tornado. When he finishes, he begins to sand the rust off its side.

Emery for the first time curses under his breath. A flare of something like rage is written in his face. I mean to ask about the repair itself, of course, but I stop myself. Instead I make some comment about the great height and the danger the repairman is in, fifty feet off the ground.

"He would do better to fall" is the reply, fairly spit out of Emery's mouth. "This is why we make no progress."

Does he mean to say that repairs are not progress? I ask precisely this question. But Emery has clammed up, I think with embarrassment at his own outburst, and to spare him I ask no more.

We continue along the river. As we walk, cows' bellies swell up above the water, the udders are rubber gloves of dainty size at this distance, splayed and covered in flies of a vermillion celluloid. A hoof protrudes. An ear with a tag affixed. The cows must have been up the Rye Valley, where, Emery claims, the silos of feed pour their foam and silage into the surface. That surface is the only thing intact and it has given way to all manner of farm equipment, the floating pail, the separator's coil...I picture the bells of the cows pulled from their necks, the bells aglide for a moment before slipping under the surface, poised in the act of sinking, between the bottom of the river and the sky above, just like copper involutions of the daylight, without casting shadows.

"Would this be the kind of place you would like to spend your life in after you are no longer alive?" I repeat my question.

Instead of an answer, he busies himself with cleaning his binoculars.

We soon find a higher vantage and can see through the surface of the Rye to what, had they been near, those people in the apartments might have seen. There are dioramas in there, shadows furred brown with minnows. Emery says you can go under the surface of the water and look through the observation windows but that we are out of time.

Later, I return to Emery's reaction with respect to the worker and the tornado. I try to suss out the rage of this unknowable man. The question of presentation looms in the background. He is angry on account of an ideal, that the Diorama of the Town could be perfect if only the other workers would see fit to try. There has been a failure of this perfection owing to a collapse of presentation. The evidence is all around, in the decay and in the failure of conservation to keep pace. But implicit in this conviction, and I admit Emery confessed to no such opinion, is the idea that the Town could, and should, be even more comprehensive and (by way of its scope and execution) perfect than it already is. What is lacking is the will to move fully to the belief. The Town could progress, but it did not, and such people as the little man at the top of the ladder were to blame.

He seemed to be saying we must conserve the Town, even as it is being expanded, before it is lost forever.

Ceremony

WHEN WE ARRIVE AT THE Galbraithe Station, Mr. Emery takes us immediately to a slab of concrete bearing the imprint of Goll's shoe and crest. All around are dedication plaques of contributors and luminaries to commemorate the completion of the Resort. In the concrete is an imprint dainty, and well-formed, and Goll's weight had pressed a knurl all around the edge. He had claimed to be a strong man, and yet, his foot is immaculate and small. And next to this is a littler shoeprint, said to be that of his daughter. But I believe the child's footprint belonged to someone else, someone else's child, perhaps the winner of a contest, the prize of which was to meet the great Minister Goll and make an imprint at the dedication ceremony. Goll had no real children. His interactions with children were all staged. Children terrified him.

Cable

A CABLE CAR FERRIES US up Galbraithe Mountain. In the mountainside everywhere are little doors. As we climb the whistling hypotenuse of the cable, I spy a little door in the mountain, painted the color of the surrounding landscape. You can see the doorknob painted green.

Below, things speed backward greenly. A wolf pack stands in the clearing amidst the little trees you often see under cable cars, having sprouted in the open. Several members of the pack are looking up at us.

Soon, the edges of the Resort come into view. Leaning out as a ledge. We cross above the typical gardens you might expect. An effusive topiary, at once stern and almost maddening, made of the artificial hedge animals, fox, badgers, and now, elegant women and men stand in groups on pathways in the side of the hill. Every figure in evening wear. Waiters stand on the winding paths in even the most distant places, carrying trays of flutes. I imagine I see the bubbles in the champagne, but it must be my own fatigue put them there.

We climb and climb. The skylights are unnervingly close, and night is coming on. Spreading to the left, outdoor gambling on elaborate playing wheels, whose numbers had been painted to affect the blur of their spinning, go by. Male and female courtesans stand about, and later in the rooms one can observe all manner of exchanges among them and the guests. The Resort is said to be a reminiscence of a time that Goll had heard about but had not experienced, the days when Michaux was alive. To get the thing right, Emery says, historians had been consulted and afterward found themselves in the diorama.

Emery

WE DINE IN A LUXURIOUS room of chandeliers and heavy drapes, tied back. Men and women gesture around the perimeter as if watching a dance. I miss the intimacy of the train. There is a hush within the hotel, and a sense of its great size all around us. Mr. Emery, too, is quiet. He sits up straighter and seems uncomfortable. I wonder if the opulence disturbs him, and ask him if Galbraithe Resort were part of his usual "route." He replies in the negative.

"So this is your first time here also?"

"Yes, sir, it is."

"And what do you make of it."

Without hesitation, he says, "It's the most beautiful place I've ever seen. I only wish—"

He stops himself. He opens and closes his eyes several times, rapidly, with a disturbed expression that, perhaps due to our long travels and the wine, he is unable to hide. I ask him, what is it he wished; what did he mean?

He begins to tell me about his sister who had passed away and who was awaiting placement in the Town. He tells me that, when his route allows, he goes to where she is being stored and that he is "saving up" to be beside her. He says he wants to "come to rest" with her in a place they had agreed on, come what may. He had even undergone consultation with a dioramist: the pose, the sort of period clothing, the price structure. You see, the siblings had always wanted a small farm of their own, three or four cows and one or two cash crops requiring not too much labor. An apple and peach orchard, and for early fall, potatoes and carrots to keep and sell. He speaks at great length of the place.

And so they would appear, brother and sister, as a dairy maid and dairyman, respectively. They would stand in the pasture, holding hands. Indeed, there was already a dairy farm in the Seventh Ward, and it was decided that with a small deposit and monthly payments, Emery too would be located next to the young woman, when he died and Sarah was out of storage.

I am appalled, yet I check myself. Mr. Emery has become emotional, his eyes glazed but never running over with tears. I see then that he is a kind of stoic, and he has what every stoic desires, and that is a simple aim to follow. I feel I see who he is at that moment, and he, me. I wish him the best of luck in putting together the remaining details. He says, as to savings, that it will take ten years and, he repeats, that in the meantime his sister is being stored in a warehouse near the Seventh Ward. She will take the place of the young woman already standing there, who had entered the diorama against her will.

Home Dioramas

IT SEEMED THE HOME DIORAMA is not enough for Mr. Emery. I say as much. Emery says he wants more.

But people require rooms. Even families with no rooms to spare dedicate a nook or an entire room to a loved one. Note this grandmother with her sewing machine and her free weights. Her beloved dog sits beside her, as if for the viewer; he has been kept in storage until the time of her passing. Here is a little baby in a crib with a cap on, sleeping with its two fists. Note the candle, kept for the most part burning. Electric candles are increasingly popular. This shrine has a dish of water with some token at the bottom, metal and shiny.

Home displays integrate with the room in many cases. Here, we have a severed desk in the corner, emerging from the wall to save space, and the loved one, a woman, having just turned to regard the doorway, an open expression on her face, the glasses at the tip of the nose.

Objects of significance abound in these displays. We can't read them, though we can guess. The dish of candy is obvious; it was her favorite kind. There is a beer mug on a shelf, filled with loose change this old man was planning to roll. This connects us to the dish of water in which doubtless that metal object is a coin, used as a Carrier. The flame of the candle and the coin in the water form wells of entrance and exit to these sacred places.

One often finds boxes and other things temporarily stacked in Home Dioramas. Or laundry folded on the surfaces, or as here, hung from a line, to be removed when dry.

Home Dioramas II

EMERY ASKS ME DID I ever have a little diorama, a little shrine, growing up? I tell him that in the home of an uncle of mine there was always a sort of room, toward the side of the sitting room in an alcove, where the matriarch, my great-grandmother, sat in her laboratory (which had been recreated), looking through a microscope. All round her were the items of her work. Slides and so forth, flasks and jars. And books. And a gooseneck lamp, so like an undersea creature looping itself over the sample of a squirrel's head, dissected and peeled open, actually hinged open. As a boy I was fascinated by that pert instance of gore. My grandmother's right hand was poised over a notebook in the act of drawing the microscope view: bubbles, I think, in one of many references to the office of Michaux. Her beloved dog, Sparker by name, curled on the office cot, as if under a great weight.

As time went on and in humid weather an odor would arise, especially on summer holidays when the family would gather. An indescribable odor, not quite gloves or mothballs but of some sort of mysterious resin, hidden underneath, would creep into the house and over the dishes of the potlach on the long table, while my grandmother examined the biopsy of the squirrel.

Still, I found myself returning to the room again and again. I would stand at the entrance; the velvet cord touched me about mid-sternum, and I leaned in toward the artifact of the entire room, my grandmother.

Also, in a side room slightly larger than that one, there was my grandfather, frozen in the act of mounting a butterfly on its pin.

He had pierced it through the back, and in an attitude of placid concentration was about to affix the specimen to its box, in which there were twelve or thirteen other species, spread broad in a kind of forlorn magnificence, both dun and sparkling at once. They were fritillaries of one kind or another, I later learned, with an array of brown speckles on an orange ground.

His jacket hung from a hook, and he wore a homemade lab coat from one of the pockets of which projected the end of a wooden ruler. About him stood the usual stuff of the hobby entomologist. He had a row of reference books. He had a net, a mesh cage, and in it, silkworms consumed the dark mulberry leaves.

I watched him for some time, and each time I returned as I grew older, my grandfather seemed smaller, despite his fresh preparation. I was given to understand he had passed away less than a decade before. In any event, I thought I must watch him. Of that I was certain. Of all the people in the house, from the perspective of a boy, he was the most interesting. I knew he was not alive. And yet I knew that he was.

One day, when I was about seven or eight, I had gone to see him while the adults were carrying on in the other room. At once, I smelled the telltale fumes of alcohol over my shoulder, and before I could turn around, where my mother was sure to be, she said, "The old goat always did like to keep busy," and then she messed up my hair.

When I turned, my mother wore a curious expression, a sort of humorous twist to her mouth. But I didn't understand. For my grandfather *was* busy. He was very busy indeed, there with his butterfly, which was always, it seemed to me, a little closer to the final place that had been set out for it.

Thus it is that Michaux occurs again and again in our houses. Every room strikes me this way now. Every room is an artifact of something that has happened. There is still something of a cottage industry in the design and outfitting of these spaces. As well as in their restoration, or removal and storage.

I remember that day (not a week before she'd go away for good) my mother gave me my own cake, perfectly sized for a boy. I ate it by myself while the adults carried on. It had a single candle.

X: THE FINAL EVENING

The Pigeon

THE HEAT POURS UPWARD, SMELLING of newspapers and honey. The one-eyed pigeon circles a building that stands at the center of a distinct odor. It is a white building of small squares, made entirely of beehives. She can get stung, she knows, by the furred creatures exiting and entering the terraces, down-stepping. The bees enter and exit thousands of holes worn to naked wood by their bodies. All over the city, the bittersweet vine blooms white, clotting every wire, every pole a blue-white foam, congealed by distance to a false meringue. She passes the hives once again, and a building of reflective squares sections its glamour and defines her and erases her in each pane. And behind the image in the mirror outward, above the city, a great cloud, moving fast, growing larger, a boiling purple fitted with red beads, beads that are eyes, disappearing when she passes over a plaza of fountains competing for archways and splendor, and other pigeons, specks walking in circles down there, are unaware of the overpressure of a great flock, coming this way.

These are the other pigeons, the passenger pigeons. The shadows on the plaza are long. They nearly reach the vendors and the crumb-scattering people, and a mime or two: all disappear as another tower intervenes in the view, and without warning, the companions that had been following her are gone.

A quiet falls over the city. She flies alone. As through a gauze behind which she can almost see, the world has gone still. On instinct, she rolls as if the shape following behind were almost upon her.

In the silence, that magnet in her mind has fallen away. She is untethered. There is no farm. There is no home, only a hole like a cavity in the water, to swim through. Her gills open. Everywhere the slicks of her fellows strain in a current that would reject them backwards, into the hyperborean beginnings of water, into the mushrooms in roots and the long, double lines going into the dark beside the third rail. No sky, and foremost, no barn. No place, no eaves, no wire. The sound of the passenger pigeons builds to a roar, swimming in the air toward a new tower: the hidden tower behind the others.

Workshop

On our return journey to Station White and the city, Mr. Emery avoids me for the most part and discontinues our evening libation, but whether he does this in the pursuit of his duties or in the lesson of his misgivings, I do not know. To share is sometimes to be alienated.

Just that morning, we had visited the workshops and the prop warehouse under the Resort, far underground. Freight trains were often coming and going. I liked to watch them, standing at the window of my resort room, wondering what they carried.

In the warehouse the workers were away. Silence spread over the many worktables, row on row coming into being as Emery turned on the lights of the workshops.

People of all kinds and shades find their way, cold packed, to the worktables. Their skins are taken off and preserved. Their frames, their carcasses are discarded (usually taken to one of a number of piggeries on the outskirts of our city). Or they are composted by facilities at the Farmers College. The raw skeletons are put to fresh use as bone meal in the agricultural sector, and the teeth can be found, here and there, in a building top field from time to time. Children—and some adults— make a game of collecting them.

The taxidermy molds over which the skin is stretched are fashioned of wood and, more often nowadays, of resin, the latter poured into a mold and hardened to shape, the former fashioned into rough form by a lathe and router and the finishing touches done, when detail is essential, by hand. At the end of all this, one trickiness remains: for a while, every specimen looks eerily similar. There are only so many molds and positions people can be expected to hold. And they come off as too proper, almost. Their arched, dancer's backs give them the feel of imminent music, as if a waltz were about to strike up. Because of this, an articulating dummy, half armature, half mold is now used. Emery pointed one of these figures out. It lay stretched on a table. Even the radius of the prone dummy rotated over the ulna. Each of the toes were little balls connected by metal and spring-loaded tendons, a toenail carved at the end for good measure. The jaws could open and close. The teeth are blindingly white and the wood almost glows as if lacquered.

But as for the skins, as I say, people of all hues arrive at the workshops. Features are altered, hair replaced. The skins have a tendency to darken over time, both due to oxidation and as a result— depending on the person—of a natural return to their original hue. A universal dye lightens them until they are the color of oatmeal left out on a countertop. In extreme cases, they are retreated with a prophylactic intended to block the oxidizing light and air, and in the oldest specimens a paint is used.

Prop House

WE DESCENDED FARTHER INTO THE prop warehouse. In no other place, save the museum basements, have I seen so many shelves: large and small, stepping back into the dark, such that the aisles seemed to close themselves by distance alone. We rode a little picking cart which could rise up to the topmost shelf and which had a bin in the front to place the props in. Bins and bins of period doorknobs in glass, brass, nickel, and the like. Entire rows, each half a mile long, of doors, labeled and numbered. Windows, too, of every design and even of designs I had never seen and which I suppose were meant to invoke the future. Drapes packed in mothballs. Racks and racks of dresses, suits, belts, bales of ties bound with string. Carefully bundled grasses and small plants in protective cages. There was a section entirely of fire escapes like enormous insects and manhole covers with different stampings: Water, Electric, Gas. I can't describe to you the extent of the prop house. There were chicken coops, splattered and streaked, stacked on huge shelves. There were hundreds of carriages of all sizes. Bins of wedding rings. Aged work gloves. Parts for artificial trees of every species imaginable. The leaves were held in book-like pages, to be applied to twigs.

These props, as distinct from landscape features created in the workshops, came from parts of the city that had been dismantled and from which the people had been moved to make way for some public works project or other. It appeared that nothing was too insignificant to escape storage. Mr. Emery turned off each section of lights as we passed, and the darkness spread out behind us, interrupted only by racks of bulbs that were very high up and never turned off.

Cycles

During the elections, calls to "Tear Down the Sheds" were rampant, as if such a project could be done in an afternoon. It is more likely that any dismantling of the Town will take a very long time, indeed. Decades are possible. One can picture the morning and the first workers. A few, first clangs, and the machines starting up. Gradually, the human specimens and the animals will be removed from the Town, and one by one, they will go into storage and the landscape will resemble a stage after the curtain has fallen and the props people are taking away the inessential scenery, lamps, the chair the protagonist sat in, a rug, the deaccumulation of which comes as a slow shock. How empty the thing really is. The great set will remain, standing there in undeniable silence, for a while. And then it, too, will be done.

The storage of all the specimens will require a zone one-third the size of the original Town, so decisions will have to be made with respect to discard and preservation. These "little scenes," which were everywhere and which no curation could possibly encapsulate, we will be freed from. Their ordinariness. You felt you lived their lives in the split second of the encounter. And all of their lives occurred at the corner of the gaze, could scarcely stand up to scrutiny and yet were more real than you, than I, than the people they had been before they were brought here. There are no words to describe this. And there was something even more striking: if you could get the proper mindset, it was possible to rest here...

But as for calls to dismantle the Town, what of Emery's sister? I imagine her in place, in the landscape. I imagine figures standing all around, and one of them his sister. Then she is gone. The price has risen. Emery by now is an old man. He has nearly saved up. Then the landscape, far away, lightens as the shed roof is slowly dismantled. Then the buildings are torn down. They are rebuilt. As farms. As apartments covered in farms. Trees will be broken up and their steel mesh melted. And then soil trucked in and the trees and shrubs that were in evidence a thousand years ago replanted. This project will determine the inevitable dismantling of the sheds. They will daylight the River Rye.

In time the rain will fall.

In time the animals will be introduced into the new neighborhoods, and like the creatures of the city, they will be versions, they will be essays of animals. The silver-eared deer mimicking the mechanical deer designed to show it how to behave. The problems will be fixed, I have no doubt. The fox that walks backward. The wild horse that jumps up and down on its four hooves, giving little screams, will give way to calmer iterations. Something new entirely will develop from the squirrels that move only twice a day, to turn their heads in the trees, all at once. This too takes time and is taking time as we speak. We will get there in time. And the city may well resemble what it was, or something new, and yet ordinary. We will get there. And isn't that the exquisite promise? There is still hope for a newness to come again and for the angles of the buildings and their glass to be free of beforetimes. For the rain to fall at an unprecedented angle.

The Offering

THE TRAIN SLOWS, THE SHEDS step downward out the window. There, in the haze, stands Station White, from which we departed ten days past. How small it looks as we approach, just a diminutive station, in marble aged black by the smokestacks in the distance. An attendant collects my luggage. Emery stands very near to me, as if he is afraid I might have a fall at some sway of the car. To both sides the last remaining streams of the Diorama of the Town pass over the surface of the windows.

And a little white rectangle appears out of the corner of my eye.

"Sir, I would like to present you with this."

Mr. Emery bends toward me, intent and very focused on some idea within himself. At the end of his hand is a small card: M. Entren, Consultant in Taxidermy, Bonded, Insured, it read. This is the person whom Emery had used to design his, and his sister's, taxidermy. Mr. Emery intimates that, should I wish to appear in the Town, it is very, very possible. That (and what he says next surprises me) "Economies of Scale," especially the pooled monies of those people retiring from work, will help ensure everyone will have the chance, one day.

One day. The phrase, unspecific as to time, sticks in my head. I feel sorry for him, and in the unique reversal of such moments, he feels sorry for me. But he hasn't been forced to offer me the card. He is doing so out of kindness. His face is pained, there is a desperation writ there, on my account.

The train car aisle holds still. The outside world vanishes. No picture of it remains. Something beyond the physical is occurring. I have, Emery is saying, this one chance to live. And though perhaps he isn't aware, this is a gesture of spiritual, of metaphysical, despair, for me, for himself. My heart goes out to him. Kindness takes the strangest forms. And after all, what do I know, having not really earned, but simply survived into, old age?

It is the tentative way he holds the card that gets me. His whole body leans forward and almost curves around the offering. I know he is a shy man and that a gesture such as this is, for him, unprecedented. He has been saving the possibility of sharing this information, but he never believed he would take himself up on it. And now, here he is in what, in other circumstances, I might have seen as absurd. But this is the bridge, is it not? The double need, by another rubric, on the shore you will cross to, indistinguishable except for this moment when you, too, have some necessity of belief, will get you, too, one day. And a deep superstition tells you that the mirror can be cruel if you do not now be gentle.

And yet, it is more than this. I have made Emery fully less. I confess it. Some smallness in me cleaved to him then. His scheme and its hopes are mad, but the absurd is no protection against fellow-feeling. We can only approach with our refusal. Or our acceptance.

I take the card and thank Mr. Emery. And in that moment I really do think I have every intention of calling M. Entren, Consultant in Taxidermy, Bonded, Insured. The train has come to a stop. The door roars open down the aisle, and for the first time I smell, as one does in a building, the rain outside. I wish Emery the very best.

I hate goodbyes.

Return: Department Store Windows

THESE ARE STRANGE DAYS, JUST after my return. I am passing by the Nelson Department Store windows in the early morning, on my way for some jam at a nearby shop, and there in the dark dawn, along the sidewalk, softly in the dark, are the advertisements in their glass enclosures. Dioramas, all. An unease comes over me. I think I see there all the lineaments of the Town. The canoe of the father and daughter: the brown trout suspended with their speckled sides, the girl pointing downward, "There, Daddy, see the fish!" and the sigil of the fingers, a gestural echo from before, yet broken as to the deep thematics of the Town, surviving here nonetheless, as a visual sound. One by one, the displays pass, splendors in the dying nighttime. You feel stars. They gather the stars around them. When I reach the square, the kiosks are just rolling up and the lights going on in the quiet of the first nicker and the first hooves coming out of the walls as if from elsewhere, perhaps behind me, and as I reach, a jellyfish, or a globed apartment, drifting as a satellite beyond the veil, in the great Elsewhere, I remember, as I pull the jar off the shelf, that I have seen this very brand in the Town.

And in the ensuing week, going about the city in the disposition of my day, going about the streets in the hubbub and clangs of sound, trying to decide if I should call on Jeffrey, I can't tell whether I wish all the people and things to be stilled forever or to remain as they are. This is a kind of desire, the clattering silences going out like the shutter of a camera in all the distances, though our city always feels like it's empty, doesn't it. That's its design. Ours is a city poised at midnight where you can buy jam in a forest. Later, I apprehend such a choice as a schoolboy's fancy when really, Jeffrey, isn't it more likely that an intolerable mix of the two stretches between moment and moment like a velvet cord?

Twinning

THAT IS WHAT THEY ARE saying, these two, Michaux and Goll. These things had already been done, been seen, at the very beginning, before or after these people, and these animals had been chosen, by accident or on purpose. That was Goll's game, positioned outside. For his part, Michaux had come to the things of the inner world.

But every dioramist is the same person, as every diorama is the same and every figure the same person, containing the shape of the same woman, the same man, employing the methods of fiction. Every dioramist is a twin. I feel my faith breaking.

Michaux and Goll stand together in the excerpted world. The same methods. The same whim. Exchange one bird for another. They are entangled in the same flock. Only the intention is different. I have been searching for patterns. And earlier still, I had thought to find the image of the lone worker, separated from community. But a spell has come over me. I do not want those things anymore. I don't even care about them. As the thematic Town overtakes me in the days after, I want, quite simply, leaning forward, holding my breath, to see again what has been done. I want the methods of fiction. A simple trip. To rest awhile in the totality. A tour. It's come to that.

I am a tourist.

Amateur

IT IS NEARLY DAWN. IN my guest room I stand for a while. For the past three weeks I have gotten rid of one diorama a week, placing it on the curb. One remains, the theen finches, which have turned blue. The forest floor gathers the wet, going out into the blackness. I hold it in my hands. Then I ride the elevator down. I place the diorama on the curb and return to my balcony.

Dawn comes. A soft thump behind the wall: Carla is up. A sneeze: Tom, who has not gone to sleep. I go to the railing. Three floors down, the neighborhood cats approach the finches carefully. I watch to see who will come and claim the diorama. The previous week, an old woman had carried away the rats, and the week after, a girl of about twelve had taken the turtle with the grasshopper in its mouth. But this morning no one comes. I finish my tea as the sun rises into the canyon.

When the garbage collector arrives, he pauses at the diorama. Taking off his cap, he wipes his brow with his forearm. Hands on hips, he looks down at the diorama. He lifts it and holds it in front of him, out at the end of his arms, as if he would try it on. Then he puts it carefully on the wagon-bed and clops on.

Seeing

THE DIORAMA IS A WAY of seeing that the entire world orients on, as well as the extinction of a way of seeing: that is the hidden pain and has been all along, when we intuited the end at the very beginning of our sight. This, until we work out a new way, will be the engine of every conflict. But don't be afraid. There is still time to pretend to a beginning.

Because there *is* still time. I was just walking along with Jeffrey the other evening. And the buildings, like great ovens, showed their brief innards. A head passes. A set of elbows under a blind. Those lenses step upward and to the left and right as across a blue carpet. This is the song of nostalgia, and of elegy as well, and we must train ourselves not to listen too much. That too carefully we turn its globe, still orange and interpolating in the dark, and roll and blow the shape to the ends of the groundform world itself, is a kind of elegy.

Genetics

THIS MORNING A DEER—ONE OF the non-mechanical ones—passed behind me as I stood at the Nelson. I saw it reflected in a window, its one leg up, ear twitching, watching me.

I remember when Mr. Emery took me to the Lookout Post on Galbraithe Mountain, just before our departure. We looked west, where we had not been. As far as the eye could see, the landscape of the Town swept on, into the bright mists you often see in vast indoor places There was no end that I could see. The Town went on, ready for new buildings, many of which were under construction. You could see the little foundations, boxed out.

In the middle of an open space there was a tiny green tube, like a cigarette in the distance, lying on the ground. It was a carpet of artificial grass that hadn't been rolled out yet. Antlike figures walked around it, and machines. I put a coin in the telescope: there was a herd of deer off to the side. Two tiny men were tearing off the protective wrapping. Where they would go remained to be seen.

In the Room

THE PHONE RINGS.

Gripping the receiver, I listen intently. It is Emery, I am sure of it. Emery on the other end of the line. At some hidden telephone, set into a plaster cliff of the Town. The train has stopped. He has stepped off, and he is alone and calling me. He is calling to tell me something he'd meant to say. But no one speaks. The card he has given me lies beside the phone. The card I will never use.

Across that howling line, scenes form. Birds hop in the Town. They disappear in a hedge. But then they are in the city. The wind blows by virtue of the shape of the trees. The starlings. They all rise. In a wave they settle back down, the shape of an intention. Inside and outside, Emery is holding his breath. He has seen his error. For an instant, I believe he's had a change of heart.

He is just about to tell me.

Forward

MICHAUX SAYS WE BECOME NOSTALGIC for the future and for the idea that there could be a future at all.

He says, for there to be a future there must be nostalgia for events that have not happened and that will consist in our absence and that we will never see. We will gather purity to us by our absence from the world. That is the hope, anyway. The diorama thus presents us with a picture of the end of the world, with ourselves as the final viewer in a place, our own world, that has ended.

When I was little, when we would cross a street, I would hold onto my mother's finger. She was an exacting woman. The rain had to fall a certain way. If it did not, she would pull me into shelter wherever it could be found. And so it was that we had come into the museum to get out of the rain, and as I smelled the wet wool of her coat and the leather of her purse, we stood in the dark, dripping. The whole veldt was poised in the lighted space before us. Something, it seemed to me, was about to happen, was about to be done, if only we stood long enough.

Origin

THE ONE-EYED PIGEON PREPARES TO leave. When she was young, she circled the barn in the city, following the other city pigeons for another round. But this day, she reaches, as if she were following a spoke of the sky from a center hub; she reaches too far. She reaches past. The other pigeons flying with her pull at her, pulling her back to them, yet they follow her in a deviating path. The magnets in their heads begin to pain them; they are not meant to come this far. Their minds begin to cloud with an anxiety that has no name, with a physical tearing in which nothing is torn. This is the farm, pulling them toward its well, and they fall away and fade, rejoining the wheel. And the one-eyed pigeon flies on alone.

In the distance the passenger pigeons darken the sky. They arrive in the city in a deafening roar. They are coming toward her. The city ripples and heaves below. A great wave rises over the earth. As cats and dogs, as rats and mice lift from the ground, as two or three deer try to run in the sky, as horses and farm and city people become light and drift upward with buildings and towers and bridges. They are exiles. They are pulled along. The grey bodies, the alert red eyes of the passenger pigeons utterly foreign to the one-eyed pigeon whose homing instinct begins to be stretched like a gum band causing a flutter in her mind exactly like the last current of energy through the body of a dying fish. And then it breaks, all at once. The center point of her locality, which went on under the eaves, in the cupola and winging round these two pivots as the turning world, floats away, a hoop tossed by a child, and all around, the galloping of wings.

She rises. Below, grey wheels of similar birds, pigeons like her, turn over the squares of the city, left behind. Homing pigeons. She already doesn't remember, yet when she kicks her wings, rising yet higher, trying to keep up, a barrel in her guts turns over, and she knows for an instant this is her place, home in the bones, and then the awareness, more a memory of the nose than the eye, passes, and she's off again. Only, it seems a similar wheel has gotten into her, and she's turning as if to tack. The barn where she was born comes into view, the green crops surrounded by the city blocks, and the tug of home rearranges every part of her mind. She remembers.

Panic overtakes her. She strains to go back. But the flock in its mass is at full speed. They are faster than she, the passenger pigeons, stronger, larger. They fly with a maddening speed. All around her, the unfamiliar bodies—their black-necklaced heads, their red eyes— regarding her (and she saw them long before, in the forest, covering the ground, devouring chestnuts bulging their throats as they go down, as if she were a simulacrum and an extensive ghost in their foreignness, surrounded on all sides as, flying, she stepped through the leaves, the iridescence of her throat startling now one, now one hundred, heads popping up, which one after another resume, downward, their pecking of the ground as if they were as many corks on a wave just passed), and before she can register anything of a decision, the one-eyed pigeon has streaked across the border of the final wheel, and the sound of bird-strikes into building-sides in the fog of other birds, ahead and to the side, and the flock bends ahead, around a leaning structure she just misses. Those behind her collide, a rumbling of birds.

The city, her city, seems familiar in the glimpses below. Its contours, its odors. The cries, the newspapers flapping in the squares on the breeze. Only, there are no people there, and no squares, no papers. The land opens. She quickens her flight, just as if she were aware, as if something were chasing. She is migrating away. She is a passenger.

About the Author

BLAIR AUSTIN WAS BORN IN Michigan. A former prison librarian, he is a graduate of the Helen Zell Writers' Program at the University of Michigan where he won Hopwood awards for Fiction and Essay. He lives in Massachusetts. *Dioramas* is his first novel.